THE DAWN OF DOOMSDAY

I read over the print-out again. There was no mistake. My head swam. I'd invented these formulae only as part of a make-believe universe; I'd never dreamed they'd be anything else. I had used real-universe data as my starting point. And here was a print-out telling me that my time-travel formulae might apply to the real world as well.

I grabbed my overnight bag and packed my notebooks and computer programs. Then I wrote the word "OHIO" on a piece of scrap and left it on Worm's bed as a clue.

I stopped at the bank and withdrew a hundred fifty dollars of the money intended for next term's tuition. Minutes later, I was on a bus—bound for Ohio and the famous Professor Terence Miller. . . .

THE GADGET FACTOR

"Will hold the attention of anyone interested in computers and provides insight into the emotional world of the child prodigy."
—*Christian Science Monitor*

SIGNET Science Fiction from Mike Resnick

THE
GADGET
FACTOR

by Sandy Landsman

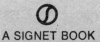

A SIGNET BOOK

NEW AMERICAN LIBRARY

PUBLISHER'S NOTE

This novel is a work of fiction. Names, characters, places, and incidents either are the product of the author's imagination or are used fictitiously, and any resemblance to actual persons, living or dead, events, or locales is entirely coincidental.

NAL BOOKS ARE AVAILABLE AT QUANTITY DISCOUNTS WHEN USED TO PROMOTE PRODUCTS OR SERVICES. FOR INFORMATION PLEASE WRITE TO PREMIUM MARKETING DIVISION, NEW AMERICAN LIBRARY, 1633 BROADWAY, NEW YORK, NEW YORK 10019.

RL/IL6+

This is an authorized reprint of a hardcover edition published by Atheneum Publishers, and published simultaneously in Canada by McClelland & Stewart, Ltd.

SIGNET VISTA TRADEMARK REG. U.S. PAT. OFF. AND FOREIGN COUNTRIES
REGISTERED TRADEMARK—MARCA REGISTRADA
HECHO EN CHICAGO, U.S.A.

SIGNET, SIGNET CLASSIC, MENTOR, PLUME, MERIDIAN and NAL BOOKS are published by New American Library, 1633 Broadway, New York, New York 10019

First Signet Vista Printing, April, 1985

1 2 3 4 5 6 7 8 9

PRINTED IN THE UNITED STATES OF AMERICA

To Mom and Dad, with love

Contents

1 Opening Moves

My parents were pretty proud of me the day they loaded up my worldly belongings and sent me off to Franklin College. At thirteen, I was the youngest in the state's history to be admitted, and I even got my picture in the celebrated *Great Neck Record;* I'm sure Mom sent clippings to all the relatives.

I was pretty glad myself—maybe the classes would keep me awake for a change, and maybe the other guys in class would know what I was talking about for a change, too. I didn't tell my parents, but mostly I was just glad to be getting out of that house at last and away from them. I think I'd have been glad to go to Siberia, if you want to know the truth. Sure, they were proud of me—sometimes. But they were also always on me for one ridiculous thing or another, every little thing I did wrong. Even when they said something good, it was kind of backhand. "You can remember all these wonderful mathematical formulae—so *why* can't you remember to put your socks in the laundry bin?" And then she'd wring her hands, to be sure I knew what a trial I was to live with. As if the world would rise or fall because I left my socks on the floor or wore them an extra day. "When you go away to school, no one will be around to *tell* you to change your socks. Your roommate won't tell you. What will you do *then?*" I think that's what clinched it for me to apply.

Anyway, Dad took the day off from work, and they drove me out to Franklin, brought up my bags, and treated me to lunch and last-minute parental admonitions. Not knowing any better, we ate at the school cafeteria, which is about two steps below prison food. Mom and Dad had what passed for roast beef in a murky gravy, and I had a tuna sandwich with catsup, which is still the way I'll eat most forms of protein— eggs, cheese, turkey, whatever, it has to have catsup on it or I won't eat it.

"Now you remember your room number?" were Mom's almost final words. "It's a big place, so don't get lost."

"And *he's* a big boy," said Dad. "He'll man-age." He grinned down at me, as if I should be grateful and pleased, like when a kindergartener gets told he's a "big boy." I think he just chalked it up to my general strangeness when I didn't respond. As a point of fact, I'm small and young-looking even for my age.

"Well, I hope so," said Mom. "You know we're all *very* proud of you. Now don't forget to call!"

I managed the amazing feat of finding my room again. Of course I'd never tell her, but Mom was right: I *could* have forgotten the room number—

I hate wasting my time on trivial little things like that, and someone else usually remembers anyway. This time I lucked out; I hadn't had time to lose the envelope with my key in it yet, and the room number was printed right on the envelope.

Anyway, my room was in a new cinderblock building, with suites made up of two rooms each. Each *A* room had one occupant, and each *B* room had two.

When I walked into the suite, a tall blond guy was sprawled out on the floor of the *A* room, lettering some tag board with a marking pen. So far he had written only the word "KILL," in crimson letters. I decided he was probably a political type, perhaps a little overenthusiastic.

"Hi. I'm Michael Goldman," I said.

He looked up and smiled. "Glad to meet you. I'm Buzz." He spoke with a midwestern twang. "You helping your brother move in or something?"

"No. I don't have a brother."

"Oh." Buzz looked puzzled. I got a sneaky pleasure out of watching his reaction.

"*I* just moved in."

"Oh. I'm sorry. I didn't mean . . . Hey, you a student here?"

"That's right. I'm in 412B."

"No kidding! Oh, well, then I guess we're in the same suite. Glad to know you."

I could tell he was dying to ask how old I was.

"You a freshman?" he asked instead.

"No, actually I'm a grad student." I said it just matter-of-factly enough that for a split-second I think he almost believed me. His jaw dropped. "No, I'm a freshman," I said quickly.

He laughed. "Okay. The whole building is freshmen, isn't it?"

"That's what I heard."

"You really going to school here?"

"Yes, I am. Is that so strange?"

He picked up on my annoyance. "Oh. Well, drop in any time." He returned to his lettering.

I walked into my own room and surveyed the pile of luggage—a trunk, a duffle, and an overnight bag, the same ones I had used when I went to sleep-away camp four summers before. At least two of the three bags were clearly redundant, when you consider the fact that I intended to live the whole term in two pair of jeans and a T-shirt. I really didn't feel like unpacking yet—or any time for that matter. I could have lived just out of the overnight bag. But I didn't know what else to do for the moment, so I began transfering items at random from the trunk to one of the two dressers. Someone else had already begun piling white socks in a drawer of the other dresser; apparently my roommate had also arrived.

I'd filled up one drawer when the door opened and in came a runty kid who was probably seventeen but looked younger—kind of skinny, with a squarish, pimply face, curly hair, and dark-rimmed glasses. He wasn't much taller than I was.

"I guess you must be my roommate," he said.

"If you're living in 412B, I am," I said as I glanced at the number on the door. "I'm Michael."

"I'm Richard. But everyone calls me Worm."

I could kind of see why. What I couldn't see was why he'd tell me. Here he was, with a chance for a fresh start, where no one would know *what* he was called in high school, and he was *telling* everybody. We really must have looked funny together. I guess whoever matched up the roommates from our preference cards must have figured that we'd be suited to each other—or else that neither of us would be suited to anyone else.

"Why do they call you that?" I asked.

"Oh, I guess it comes from bookworm or grub, or something like that." He spoke in a quick, nervous voice, occasionally stumbling over words; he'd go as far as he could on one breath, then stop wherever in the sentence he happened to be—even in midword—for another gulp of air before plunging onward. On the whole, he gave the impression of being someone from another planet who had just recently learned to speak as earthmen do and had not yet quite mastered the art. "I don't mind," he continued. "That's the way the other kids understand me."

"Is that what you want me to call you?"

"Well, it's eff—efficient. If you say Richard, you might conceivably mean someone else. But I'm reasonably certain there's only one Worm on campus."

I was reasonably certain, too.

He looked at me critically. "You skip a grade or something?"

"A few." I held back a smile—which probably made me look like a nerd, but I didn't want to seem like I was bragging.

"A *few?* How many?"

"Well, if you figure it out, it comes to five. But I kind of skipped the last few years of high school all at once."

"Oh." Worm was quiet for a moment. "I skipped one—that was all they let you do in my school."

I considered telling him that skipping grades wasn't general practice in my school either, but I decided not to. His ego looked hurt.

"Do you know what you want to study?" he asked.

"I think either math or theoretical physics. What about you?"

"Computers." For the first time I saw a spark of enthusiasm in his eyes. His voice became animated. "I've read a lot about them, and I know how they work—and I've gotten to use some micro-computers a little bit. But do you know what they've got here?" He paused for effect. "They've got an IBM 3033, four smaller models, and consoles, all hooked up into the largest center in upstate New York. You can take courses in it and then go down and use their whole system. Their whole system—can you *imagine?* Are you taking any computer courses?"

"Well, I thought about it—"

"Michael," he interrupted. "I don't tell this

to everyone. With most of the guys here, their idea of computers is probably straight out of some video arcade—they rack up a few points on Pac-Man or Donkey Kong, and they think they know computers, so what's the point of even talking, right? But if you're really serious about math and science, I strongly urge you to take at least a few basic computer courses. I'm convinced that before long computers will be *the* tool for basic research in higher mathematics and the sciences!"

He paused for breath, looking exceptionally pleased with himself. I grabbed the opportunity to get in a few words myself. "Well, as I said, I was thinking about it. I've done some reading on the subject—"

"Good! But just reading about it isn't the same. Once you get your hands on one of those . . . you'll be hooked!"

He was right. I was hooked already. Worm apparently knew more about computers than I did yet, but I too had daydreamed over the Franklin College catalog description of their computer system and course offerings. Computers intrigued me on two levels: first, for the gadget factor—the machines' technical excellence and attractiveness as a form of new toy; and second, for the smooth, irresistible logic of their operation. If you only followed the logic and provided the proper input, you could get incredible, beautiful, *certain* results. The computer was not only the ultimate gadget; it was the ultimate mind against which to test my own.

2 Universe Prime

Classes at Franklin were different from what I was used to. Back in high school, most of the teachers would let me just sit in a corner and do my own work, since I was so far ahead of the class; they'd usually try to make me participate like everyone else for the first few weeks and then they'd give up on the idea and leave me alone, which is how I liked it. So whatever grade they skipped me to for any year didn't make much difference, since I ended up doing my own work anyway. The times I liked best were when the book I was reading left something out. For instance, a few years back when they had me in seventh grade, my book on algebra asserted that quadratic equations could be graphed as sections of a cone and left it at that. Well, I took a few pieces of paper and a pencil and *proved* it. Sometimes, when I really got involved, the teacher would have to interrupt to remind me to get to my next class, and once in a while, when I was *really* involved, I'd just sit down in the hallway outside the door of the class I'd just left and finish what I was doing. The other kids thought I was really strange.

Well, as I said, things were different at Franklin. The class as a whole was a lot more on its own; if you felt like skipping a class one day, for instance, it was no big deal, no one tracked you down for it. You could skip classes all term, if you wanted, and no one could *make* you go (though they could and would flunk you for it). But, at least in the smaller classes, if you were there you'd better participate: no more solving my own problems off in a corner. That took some getting used to, but it was okay because for a change the classes were about at my level and I could talk to the other students about them— it was even kind of exciting. Even the courses in Literature, Poli Sci, and Freshman Comp, which the school said I had to take to be "well rounded," got pretty interesting sometimes. I could take two elective courses, and I had been torn among math, a science, and computers, but finally decided on Physics and Computer Science 101. I comforted myself with the knowledge that after freshman year I could take more and more of the things I really wanted to study.

Even in physics and computer science, we were pretty much on our own. Which was great. The only hitch was Dean Stanley—the Dean of Freshman and my very own personal faculty advisor. Every student had an advisor—at least in theory—but in practice it usually just meant that he signed your list of courses twice a year and got a copy of your final grades. With me it was different.

I suppose I should have been complimented— not every student gets a genuine dean as his advisor. But Stanley seemed to take his job much too seriously. He was always stopping me in the halls to "chat," scheduling little meetings to make sure everything was going okay, asking teachers how I was doing, that kind of thing. Whenever I saw him, it made me feel as if I'd never left high school. I guess I got the special treatment because I was so much younger than the others; they probably weren't quite sure I could handle being away from home without freaking out or something stupid like that. Mostly, Dean Stanley was a nuisance. I gave him five or ten minutes of my time when I had to and then promptly forgot about him.

From the first, Worm was my only real friend on campus; whoever had matched us had done a better job than I first thought. We were both younger and brighter and stranger than the other kids, and everyone knew it. Some of the guys referred to us as Batman and Robin (presumably I wasn't Batman). We didn't talk much about how that felt, but we each knew the other understood.

One day someone put a sign on our door saying, "CHILD PRODIGY TRAINING CENTER. Apply Within." We left it up for the rest of the term. Inside, we had begun to fill up the walls with absurdities—deadpan quotes from our course readings or other pronouncements that the authors evidently felt were words of wisdom. We took a gleeful excitement in finding them and competing with each other for the most outrageous examples. My favorite was one I found, a footnote from an introduction to the writings of Montesquieu: "18. According to Dedieu, *ibid.*, p. 25, Montesquieu seems to have been perplexed until about 1727."

Buzz, by the way, turned out not to be political at all. The sign he was lettering the first day, and which he hung proudly above his bed, read "Kill a Commie for Mommie." He was practicing being facetious.

Most of the guys tried to make me feel at home, but I could tell they were *trying*, kind of humoring me, not really taking me seriously. I could hold my own with anyone in rap sessions on Plato or Shakespeare, but when the subject turned to their main interests—sex and football, in emphatically that order—well, football I had no interest in, and how much could even a very advanced thirteen-year-old talk to horny college kids about sex? Any opinion I had on the subject brought forth tolerant, half-hidden smiles, as if to say, "Isn't he cute?" I hate that.

But what *really* drove me up a wall was that even though I had definite interests in the subject, none of the girls took me seriously either. Girls my own age I had no way of meeting, and even if I did, if they were anything like the kids my own age I knew from Great Neck, I wouldn't have much to talk to them about anyway. How much can you say to a girl who gets her biggest thrills in life by daydreaming over some dumb TV star or who can't look you in the eyes without giggling? College girls, I could at least talk to. There were some who really cared what I thought about our course reading or the results I got in physics lab and were impressed as hell with me—as a brain. But a lot just thought it was hysterical to hear all those words coming from a thirteen year old. I began to get the feeling I was an exhibit at some science fair, demonstrating what a real live child prodigy acts like. But when I didn't talk about something intellectual, I didn't know what to say; I mean, I really couldn't figure out what normal people talk about. So, there were about three girls I really liked, who I'd say hello to when I saw them, and the conversation would go something like this:

"Hi, Margie."

"Oh. Hi."

"How ya doing?"

"Fine. And you?"

"Okay."

Then either I'd save myself by reciting some insight I had gotten into the schoolwork or she'd ask me if I knew the answer to a homework problem or I'd just stumble for a minute and say, "See ya." She'd give me a nice smile, probably thinking of me as a puppy to be patted on the head. Then I'd go home and imagine what it would be like if she ever went on a date with me.

To put it bluntly, I was not and never had been the social success of the season. What I *was* a success at was computers. Worm and I spent more and more time at the computer center, trying test problems from further and further along in the book, making up our own problems, learning computer games from some of the more experienced students. The amount of detail that went into the programing for some of those was fantastic—absolutely incredible. Worm and I would take turns at the controls, trying to outwit each other with the absolute logic of the program. Some of the first games we learned were just souped-up video games—but soon we were playing *computer* games: games that you won by logic and strategy, not by who had the better manual dexterity or could push a button faster.

I'd never gotten into video games all that much—I mean they were fun, but I could walk away after an hour or so. But *these* games were something else. At the simpler end of the scale was a game called Moon Landing (Object: to use just the right amount of power to cushion my landing without catastrophically using too much fuel—which would show up with a computer's insane logic as a space-craft position some 150 feet below the moon's surface—that meant I had crashed). From there, games ranged upward in complexity through Dungeons and Dragons and 3-D Chess to a simulated city government, complete with its own economy and political intrigue. One game could go on for days, even weeks. I mean, it was *real*—more real than a world that produced "Dedieu, *ibid.*" on Montesquieu's perplexities, and certainly more real than sitting in classes or trying to communicate with kids who looked at you like a freak or a munchkin.

I stopped going to most of my classes, except for Physics and Computers. I think Worm stopped, too. We never talked about it, but with the time he spent in the room and at the computer center, I don't see how he could have been going much. We didn't spend much time with ordinary computer problems anymore, either; we concentrated on more and more elaborate games.

One night, lying in bed, I got a brainstorm. I was thinking about Plato's Republic—kind of an early utopia I'd read for Poli Sci at the beginning of the term—and wondered what it would be like to program on a computer the government described. I began mapping out in my mind a flow chart for a general plan of attack, when it hit me: if *this* could be programed, why not more? Why restrict it to just a plan of government? We could include an ecosystem, a whole planet . . . and more. Just a flash of an idea—and suddenly I was awake, as excited as I'd ever been. It reminded me of the time at the age of nine when I first intuited what geometric proofs were all about and set out to prove every theorem in the book in two sleepless, exhilarating nights. Only this was even better—the scope so much more sublime.

"Worm?"

"Yeah?"

"Why don't we invent our own computer game?"

He sat up in bed. I could sense a grin spreading

on his face. "Yes—yes, that would be a challenge. Very complex to do, if we do it right. I mean, unless we do another computer tic-tac-toe or something trivial like that, but if we do it right . . ."

My toes tingled. "Worm—what I'm thinking of isn't trivial."

"You thought of a premise?"

"Yes." I waited a minute, drawing out the effect.

"Well? Come on!"

"Supposing—supposing we could program our own *universe?*"

"Our own universe?"

"Galaxies, planets, the laws of physics—with just a few strategic differences from the laws of physics in this universe, that might enable, say, a practical form of time travel or whatever else we decide we'll want to do in the new universe. And one community in particular. And people—we can give them names and characteristics, set them in action . . . A whole universe in a computer!" The scope of the project floored me.

For once, Worm was silent, too. At last he laughed. "Mike, you're a megalomaniac! It's tempting—it's very tempting—but we could never do it. It would take too much time—too many man-hours for us to write the programs, too many computer-hours to test it out and debug it and set it in motion."

I was ahead of him. "We'll incorporate existing programs—every computer game, every description of the physical and social universe that's ever been programed, we'll tie them all up into the biggest game of all!"

Worm shook his head. "You're crazy—but I can't pass it up!"

I felt like jumping out of bed. "We'll call it . . . Universe Prime—*our* universe. With a Planet Miko and a village called the Worm Farm!"

"Run by a Worm who is brilliant and eccentric and true and a champion among earth burrowers!"

"And by Michael, who is strong and brave and tall and shrewd! Michael is the ruler, and Worm is his loyal helper."

"Hey!"

"Well, *I* thought of it!"

"Co-rulers. Co-rulers or I won't play."

I felt so good I conceded the point. "Co-rulers. With alternating six-month periods of ascendancy—mine first. And we'll rule benignly for our loyal subjects."

Already in my mind I was sketching out a plan of attack for the programing. The keyboard would be our instrument of control; and the print-out terminal would tell us the consequences of our actions and the fate of an entire universe—droughts, years of plenty, space travel, creatures from other worlds, the birth and death of a billion stars—all locked in the circuits of the IBM 3033. The Universe, in the mind of God.

3 Genius at Work

Of course, that last metaphor was a little extravagant, though it about sums up the excitement I was feeling. But, to be precise, the metaphor was not accurate. The computer is not a god. It is not even human. As everyone knows, or should know, computers can do only what they are programed to do. No flashes of insight, no brilliant intuitive leaps, no sudden syntheses of previously unrelated materials from divergent memory banks into an unexpected, unique whole. To put it bluntly, the more I worked with computers, the more I was finding that computers are dumb—unimaginative, routined. And *literal*-minded! If you forget to program a computer to go on to the next step, there's no telling it, "well, you know what I mean"—it just sits there, or computes as if the step never existed.

A computer will rigidly follow its own logic come hell or high water—which is why some people have a hard time coming to grips with them and why nearly everyone hates dealing with them over, say, a billing error. But that logic is also a computer's strength—logic, memory, and speed. If you can duplicate that logic precisely and harness it, you can program a "what if" to take into account hundreds of variables and thousands of memorized constants and run through any number of possible scenarios for a situation—changing one variable here, another there, in effect creating and trying out different versions of reality—and all in seconds! (Once you've done the time-consuming work of writing the program, of course.) For the first time in my life, I could have control, the ability to create my own reality, to my own specifications.

When I was younger, I used to drive my parents and teachers crazy with questions that had no real answers. What if, through some fluke, the parents of Columbus had never met? Would someone else have discovered America, at some later date? Would colonization have also begun later, and different people emigrated and married? Would our country have a whole different population and a whole different history? Or what if Einstein had died in childhood, or what if Lee Harvey Oswald had missed? Were there whole alternate worlds that could have been? And why was ours the one that actually happened?

That's what my game was all about. I set up certain laws that had to be obeyed. But within those laws, there were choices that Worm and I could make, and each choice would affect all succeeding choices. Joe might marry Cynthia instead of Abigail; the wheel might be invented a little sooner or a little later; nuclear weapons might appear at a more or less advanced stage of world political development. My goal in the game was to ensure that the planet survive and prosper; Worm's goal was to bring about its destruction.

I set to work programing my universe immediately, with Worm's help. There were so many choices to make, so many details to consider, so many different approaches to try out. Combining them all into one coherent whole was more complicated than writing a seven hundred page novel. Slowly, we could see our world taking shape before us. WORM and Michael (code-name SMIK, for super-Mike, since names at this point were limited to four characters, and for programing reasons M was not available for the first character)—WORM and SMIK took on their own distinct personalities, abilities, usefulnesses.

WORM was a creature of darkness, shadows, nighttime. He worked by unseen influences, surreptitiously substituting one variable for another, affecting changes indirectly, always working on a factor that would *affect* the desired variable rather than on the variable directly. SMIK, on the other hand, was strong and direct, a ruler of sunshine and daylight, a mover. He refashioned a program here, redefined a term there, changing the Universe Prime directly. WORM was powerful at night, from 1800 HRS to 600 HRS, ineffective by daylight; SMIK was the opposite. SMIK was the Creator, WORM the Destroyer, the unseen decay. Two forces in uneasy equilibrium. We kept programing.

After several weeks, I was missing nearly all my classes, and Dean Stanley was apparently beginning to notice; I became adept at avoiding him. I took the long way around to the computer center so I wouldn't pass near his office. I made sure never to step outside for a breather during his ten-thirty coffee break or one-o'clock-sharp lunch hour. He left phone messages at my dorm room, and little notes started appearing in my mailbox. "I must talk with you—please call!" "Aren't you attending classes now? Please call my secretary to set up an appointment." "I really must see you—urgent!" Meanwhile, UNIVERSE PRIME was proceeding apace, and if there was one thing I didn't need to be bothered with, it was Dean Stanley. I bought a little time: I returned his calls, but always at precisely 10:35 or 1:15, and left a message only that I had called. "We keep missing each other!" read the next plaintive notes. "Please make an appointment!" I knew I'd have to pay for it when he caught up with me, but at that moment I just didn't have the time to spare.

Worm and I were practically living at the computer center, existing on coffee and doughnuts. We went back to our dorm room only when the computer center locked at midnight. In our room we brainstormed and detailed further programming to try out when the center reopened at six in the morning. I was surviving on three hours of sleep at night and loving it. The tension showed, however, when Worm and I would snap at each other and plunge into screaming fights over some detail of the programing; or when we'd startle the other students with giddy bursts of laughter at some private joke we'd just programed into UNIVERSE PRIME and celebrate by battles with discarded computer cards as weapons. We both began to look like derelicts, but all in all, I'd never felt more alive. WORM and SMIK—rulers, demigods, explorers in a new universe of our own creation.

We programed a list of one thousand citizens—names, ages, family relationships, occupations, personal histories. We programed laws and folkways. We programed international politics; and, for some as-yet-to-be-decided future date, we programed the foundations of interstellar politics as well. We programed geography, ecology, star maps, even psychological profiles of the principal personalities. In playing the game, we would set our pieces in motion at the dawn of civilization and cover centuries in seconds. The object, sublimely simple: survival. A thousand daily choices would add up to one momentous result for the inhabitants of the WORM FARM and all the other communities on the PLANET MIKO in UNIVERSE PRIME: would the planet, perhaps even the universe, survive or perish? Who would win—SMIK the Creator or WORM the Destroyer?

Day by day, the program drew closer to completion. But there was still one big hitch: a time-travel function. It had been part of my idea from the beginning, but incorporating it proved to be more difficult than I'd ever imagined. Still, I re-

fused to abandon it. If I could just find a way
to allow a practical form of time travel, it would
add whole new dimensions to the game: decisions
could be changed, a choice might not *have* to
be irrevocable. PLANET MIKO might be on
the brink of destruction, but if time travel were
possible—and if the Mikans could just learn how
to use it—then perhaps they could go back to
some point before the wrong choices were made
and try it over again. They could have a second
chance, a third, a fourth. Of course, they could
destroy themselves before they even learned that
time travel existed, let alone how to use it; but
at least this way there'd always be a *chance*.

Time travel. Second chances. Simple enough
as general sci-fi concepts. The problem arose in
getting down to specifics: how to invent some
formulae that would allow for time travel and
not throw all the rest of the laws of physics out
the window. UNIVERSE PRIME could be a *little* different from the universe we live in; in fact
I wanted it to be, just for the sheer variety of
it. But I didn't want a freak show. In certain
basic ways, this universe had to be familiar and
recognizable. But every tentative scheme I came
up with had consequences that were just plain
weird—far too weird for us to deal with comfort-
ably, especially in so complex a game.

In one plan, time travel was fine and the rest
of physics worked perfectly, with the minor ex-
ception of the fact that under certain conditions
gravity would suddenly be found to work in reverse, and every person, object, and chunk of

matter on the planet would suddenly burst apart
and go hurtling into space. Another plan was
even more of a gem: the only flaw there was
that the universe had a tendency to explode and
contract about a thousand times a minute, which
didn't allow a whole lot of time between Big
Bangs for very much to happen.

It was discouraging work. I would spend days
developing a model, ironing out the bugs that
had fouled up my previous efforts, only to find
some new, still weirder problem ruining the new
one. After about five dead ends, I was almost
ready to give up on the time-travel idea entirely,
or at least save it for some other, simpler game.
That was when it happened.

It was late one night, after the computer center
had closed for the day; Worm and I were lying
on top of our beds, trying to unwind after a hard
day's programing. I was resting my eyes; Worm
was scanning through the current issue of *The
Weekly Science Review*—or actually his personal-
ized computer print-out of that magazine, cour-
tesy of Computer Reference Service. The service
was, in theory, for subscribers only, but we'd
broken the code easily and developed the habit
of plugging into it once a week or so to keep
abreast of developments in the sciences.

Suddenly, Worm let out a low whistle. "Hey,
Mike!" He laughed. "Take a look at this!"

He flung the pages in my direction. They
landed in a heap on the floor between our beds.
I picked up the print-out.

"Page six," he told me.

I scanned the page. It was filled with short, newsy items about the latest research. "Synthesis of an Elusive Protein . . . ," "Linguistic Skirmish on Chimp Island . . . ," "Tracking the Newest Comet . . ." Then I saw it—a little item at the bottom of the page, "Subatomic Particles in Time Travel?" I scanned the article quickly: something about a Professor Miller in Ohio who had observed some peculiar activity in subatomic particles and thought that it just might indicate some kind of time travel on the smallest subatomic levels. The article went on to give some particulars of the experiment and a list of sample data.

I smiled wryly. "Well, it would be nice . . ."

Worm laughed. "But not very likely."

"Hardly. I mean, this Professor Miller has undoubtedly collected some pretty strange data, but he doesn't have to haul out 'time travel' as an explanation." The concept was fine, even elegant, for a make-believe universe. But I wasn't about to start believing in time travel in the *real* world, no matter what I might wish.

"Just the same"—Worm leaned on his elbow—"wouldn't it be something if this guy were *right?*"

"Good night, Worm."

"Just a thought."

I turned out the light and lay back against the pillow, almost ready to drop off. I might have even dozed for a minute, I'm not sure, but in those few seconds, something happened. It was one of those moments when everything suddenly becomes clear, when all the little jigsaw pieces floating around in your mind suddenly fit together into one big picture. And all at once, I had it!

I snapped on the light again and reread the figures in the box at the bottom of the article. So what if the interpretation was hogwash? The *data*—the observations on which the interpretation was based—they were something else again. They were . . . well, I had to admit it: they were weird. In their own way, no less weird than the consequences of my attempts at time-travel formulae for UNIVERSE PRIME. Only these were *facts:* observed, scientific facts. And I could use them.

Worm rubbed his eyes. "What's up, Mike?"

I couldn't take time to answer. I flipped over onto my hands and knees, my heart pounding, my nose practically buried in the print-out. I took in the row of figures, then started scribbling frantically on a corner of the page.

"Mike—what is it?" I kept scribbling. "Show me!"

"I'm busy getting inspired. You can get up and look over my shoulder, if you want!"

Worm forced himself out of bed; I could sense him standing behind me in the chilly room. He didn't have a prayer of understanding my scribblings. I'd have to recopy them myself within the hour if *I* wanted to understand them in the morning. He got back into bed and pulled up the covers.

I huddled under my reading lamp with the

print-out and some scrap paper, poring over the data. I shivered a little with the cold, but I didn't care.

The data couldn't *really* indicate time travel. I was realistic enough to know that. What else *could* explain them I had no idea, and didn't at the moment care very much, either. What mattered was that I could work *as if* they meant time travel. I could take those figures as a starting point, a clever take-off, to work out yet another set of time-travel formulae of my own. And this time, if I was lucky, the only really weird consequences would be the data I was starting from.

I looked across at Worm hugging the pillow over his face, missing the whole moment. I giggled with excitement. It would work this time, it would really work. Somehow I just knew it. This time it would work.

I didn't get any sleep at all that night; I worked straight through.

By morning I had three linked equations to feed into the computer. The test was positive: the equations fit the data in the article, and they caused no major disruptions in the laws of physics.

I had invented the time-travel formulae for UNIVERSE PRIME. The game was almost ready to go.

4 Planet Miko

After that, the rest fell into place quickly. Finally it was just a matter of details and rechecking, ironing out the last few glitches so the game would run smoothly. It was maddening, having to stop and go back for the little things, the careless mistakes, just when we couldn't wait to play it. But it was necessary, and we knew it. We kept up our pace.

One morning in mid-December, as we left our suite, Buzz stuck his head through the door, bleary and sleepy-eyed.

"Geez, you guys keep weird hours!" He tried to focus. "Hey, Mike—your mother called again last night. She says why don't you answer her letters."

I grunted. Neither Worm nor I had bothered checking the mailbox in weeks; it was probably jammed with motherly epistles. Not to mention notes from Dean Stanley.

"She said, call collect. She made me promise to tell you in person. She doesn't believe you got the other messages I wrote you."

"Yeah, I got 'em. Thanks."

"So I told you." He let the door slam and headed back to bed.

I looked at Worm. "We're creating a whole universe, and she's worried about a phone call!"

It wasn't a joke. We just couldn't be bothered.

That evening, just before closing time, we debugged the last program. After nearly two months of solid work, we were ready to put our model into operation! Worm gave a totally uncharacteristic whoop; I jumped on his back and rode piggyback, while we both giggled and shouted and showered each other with powered sugar from the boxes of doughnuts that had sustained us for the past weeks. A grad student Teaching Assistant (T.A. for short) stared at us over the top of his glasses. He didn't say anything. He just stared. We stopped.

"Is this the way you always do your programing?" he asked at last.

"No, only on good days." I couldn't really stop from laughing again.

"You guys look pretty young. Are you really in school here?"

"Yeah, we're in Professor Kirstin's class." I showed him my pass.

"And is that one of his homework assignments?"

"That's right," said Worm.

"Mind if I have a look?"

"Well, it's kind of secret."

"Really? Classified?"

"Um . . ."

"You seem to be having so much fun with it. I didn't know Professor Kirstin gave such fun assignments. Let's see." He picked up the program from my seat beside the terminal and started leafing through it.

"Well, it's not exactly a homework assignment—it's more like a special project for extra credit," I lied.

He handed back the program. "Just watch it with the horseplay."

"All right."

"You guys ever think of taking a shower?"

"Hey, that's a great idea!" I shouted. "Last one in the shower's a rotten egg!" I grabbed my coat and scrambled out of the computer center with Worm loping behind me. I held the program to my chest. We were both laughing so hard we had to stop running and throw ourselves down on the frozen ground. Incredible! Tomorrow we'd actually be starting our game in earnest! It couldn't be real! Inside the lighted computer center, we could see the grad student still staring after us—as if he'd never seen two people fooling around and unwinding before.

I stopped laughing. "You think he'll do anything?"

"Nah. He must be a computer freak himself. He should be able to understand. Besides, what would he have to gain by getting us in trouble?"

"Right." The icy air was bringing me around. I began to shiver and felt a little dizzy. Worm also sobered up from his giddiness.

"Come on. Let's get back home."

The next morning, the game began.

We set the time control for some 4.6 billion

years since the formation of PLANET MIKO
and got a print-out of planetary conditions: cli-
mate, atmosphere, mineral distribution, life
forms. Then, together, we entered the information that a small band of early manlike creatures
had moved from the jungle to the shores of a
lake—and the game was on.

We zipped through the first five million years
in less than a day: tools, fire, agriculture, irrigation. Then it was time for the serious work of
developing the first cities—and beyond. The
game took on detail. A century might play out
in two minutes, or two hours. Empires rose and
fell; periods of enlightenment and discovery al-
ternated with ages of darkness and superstition.
The WORM FARM was founded, its first laws
and customs sketched out, and Worm and I bat-
tled over its fate.

Worm and I hardly spoke now, for fear we'd
let something slip. We sat at the terminal at different hours so that we could plot our next moves
without the temptation to spy on one another.
We met in passing at odd hours in our room
between programing. When I saw him, Worm
looked smug and mysterious, leaving me to imagine what nefarious moves he had in store. We
communicated by cryptic comments typed into
the computer between moves in our game—and
by messages left with Buzz. I got a secret giddy
amusement at the way he tried to cope with
us.

"Hey, Buzz!" I'd say one morning. "Tell
Worm he can expect some big doings in Quad-
rant G22X!"

Buzz gave me a long look. "Say what?"

"Just tell him—he'll know what it means!"

And then I'd disappear out the door and hurry to the computer center, leaving Buzz completely baffled.

For those first few days of the game, I was in a state of euphoria. All I had to do was sit down at the controls, and my heart started pounding. People must have wondered at my silly grin, but I didn't care. For those few days, I felt as I'd never felt in my life. Until it dawned on me that I was losing.

I really don't know how that fact could have escaped my attention for so long. True, when I first noticed it, we were still near the earliest point in history, where anything could still happen; but, just the same, if I hadn't been so entranced with the *process*, I think I would have looked a little further ahead a little sooner. Perhaps it was my playing, perhaps the game was stacked in Worm's favor from the beginning, but as the game progressed, Worm's advantage only increased.

My strategy was simple: since the Mikans' greatest dangers would be posed by modern technology, I did everything I could to speed development in other areas—political, moral, social—so that the Mikans would be better prepared to handle their technology as it developed. I fostered great moral and spiritual teachers and gave them mass followings, I endowed rulers with wisdom and common sense. Worm's task was also simple: to institute a headlong rush to technology at the expense of all the other spheres.

Worm's plans seemed to be working. No sooner did the Mikans develop tools than they used them as weapons. No sooner did they discover fire than they burned the villages of their neighbors. Mikans warred and plundered, their most inventive designs went toward instruments of destruction. At best, I was fighting a holding action, and losing even at that. If the trend continued to modern times, the Mikans wouldn't stand a chance: they'd destroy themselves within a matter of decades. Soon my whole beautiful universe would collapse; the WORM FARM, the Mikans, their discoveries and institutions, they would no longer exist. I knew it was only a game—nothing more than a series of electronic signals we had programed into a computer—but I felt the tragedy as keenly as if it had been a real world of people and children and animals about to explode into nothingness.

For two days and nights I got no sleep at all as I tested and discarded new approaches. And still Worm advanced.

We were at modern times now. Mikan scientists were finding vaccines against crippling diseases, the first tentative steps were being made toward space travel to other worlds . . . and the first crude atomic bombs were being manufactured and stored in arsenals. Mikan leaders seemed ready to use them. Now or never I must find a way to reverse the trend and set the Mikans on a safe, secure footing; if I failed now, they wouldn't have another chance—and neither would I. It was time for my last tactic.

I must reverse my entire strategy. No more

culture, no more humane politics, at least not for now; those tactics had failed. For now, I must concentrate my entire energies on shepherding the Mikans through a quantum leap in technology and theoretical underpinnings: the Mikans must develop time travel. And they must do it tonight.

It was nearly impossible; but I'd get them through it. I had to. First they must have the observations: the data that would lead them to discover time travel's existence. From there, I could guide Mikan inventors to work out the practical applications and eke out the beginnings of a second chance.

In the final hours the computer center was open that night, I instructed the computer to plug into Computer Reference Service and read through all data listed in the past ten years of *The Weekly Science Review* for position, energy, and velocity of subatomic particles. The computer was to test all data against my time-travel formulae and then read into Mikan data banks only those observations that would support the formulae and lead Mikan scientists to discover them.

It was a desperate move, and I knew it. But it was the move I'd been waiting to play. Not only to make history, but to change it. In a way, that was the power I had invented the game for. If I could just pull *that* off, then the whole game would have a meaning.

The computer center was closing. I typed frantically to finish my program. I keyed in the last few steps and scanned it over quickly.

"Closing!" the T.A. called again.

I decided that the program could do without a final check. I punched the keys to make it execute, so I'd have the print-out in the morning, before Worm could do anything else.

"Come on, it's late!"

"Okay. I'm ready."

I gathered up my notebooks and wiped the sweat from my forehead. My shirt was open to my belly button. It was hot in there, it was always hot.

The T.A. nudged me toward the door.

"Listen, Goldman, dedication is one thing, but some of us have to sleep."

"Right." At least it wasn't the T.A. who was usually on duty. This one had given me the extra five minutes I needed to finish, which was more than the other T.A. would have done. "Thanks. See you tomorrow."

I made my way through the empty hallways to the building exit. The door clicked behind me.

An icy blast cut through my shirt. My jacket! It was still draped over the chair at my console. I tried the door, but it was locked.

Well, it was too late now. It didn't matter. I'd get the jacket back in the morning. I sprinted the hundred yards to my dorm.

Music and voices filtered toward me as the elevator approached my floor. When the door opened, the hallway was filled—kids were sitting, stretched from one end of the floor to the other, talking, eating, drinking. It was a floor party—

and I hadn't even known about it, hadn't talked
to anyone, hadn't looked at the posters.

They looked up at me curiously. For a moment
I thought of sitting down for a little while, unwinding, trying out the party. But I'd hardly
seen or spoken with anyone there in weeks, and
I didn't know how to start now.

"Have a seat," came a voice from one semi-
familiar face.

"Oh, um . . ."

I didn't know these kids, I told myself. I didn't
really know them.

"Uh, no thanks. I've got work to do."

I stepped carefully among the legs and bodies
and paper plates, making my way to my room
at the other end of the hall. I couldn't take the
time, I just couldn't. I had to be up early and
make my moves, before Worm finished it all for
good. The population of a whole planet hung
in the balance, and I had to save them. It was
more than a game: it was an obligation. The Mikans needed me.

I was still a little breathless as I closed the
door; the air still felt raw in my lungs from running outside in the cold. It didn't really matter.
I crawled into bed quickly, and once I lay down,
I didn't feel like moving a muscle. Worm seemed
to be already asleep.

Lying in the darkness, I could hear the party
outside my door. Every once in a while I could
pick out a few voices floating above the rest, but
mostly it was sort of a steady hum—the sound
of a lot of people together. For a moment I felt
very alone.

5 Little Boy in the Rain

I woke up once that night, bathed in sweat. I had thrown off all the covers, but when I pulled them up again, I was shivering. I lay there like that maybe half an hour before I drifted back to sleep.

I dreamed we were starting our UNIVERSE PRIME game all over. At first the results came in the form of a printed read-out, as they really would: numbers and code words that would let us know how our world was progressing in economics, politics, ecology, energy, and a dozen other parameters. But soon the words and numbers were replaced by a video screen that actually showed the world and its people; and before long I'd forgotten about the screen too and was simply watching from inside our world. I saw the first anthropoids emerging from the forests and beginning a pattern of hunting and gathering. I saw the evolution of our species, the beginnings of language, the beginnings of agriculture, the first massive irrigation projects leading to the first cities—the first steps in the decisions of survival for our planets. At one point I saw a cave

44

family crouching around their fire, gnawing bones—and remembering to say "please" and "thank you" for passing the salt. A sudden thrill: was this the dawn of civilization? Or, it suddenly occurred to me, perhaps only its last vestiges.

But, somehow, all these scenes seemed of secondary importance. Instead, using the time-travel function, I put the machine on fast forward until I reached the main point of interest: my own life. I waited excitedly for the screen to clear. But what I saw was not SMIK the Creator, but a little boy standing in the rain—wearing a raincoat three sizes too large and nothing underneath—standing alone and thinking and getting soaked. I didn't like what I saw; as a matter of fact I was furious. I kept putting the time into reverse and going back to my childhood, changing a variable here, a variable there. What if I hadn't skipped second grade? What if I'd been in Miss Cohen's class instead of Miss Frankel's? What if I had pretended not to be so smart? What if I'd had some friends? What if I'd had different parents? But, no matter what I changed, I still came back to the same obnoxious image of the frail little boy in the rain. I screamed at my mother: "I could never do anything right! No matter what I did! It's your fault, your fault! We're going back and do this right! Don't you know we're going to *explode?*" I reached for the time control again, my hands shaking with fury—and Mom just stood there shaking her head, mumbling, "I'm sorry, I'm sorry, it's so hard with a boy like you, I'm sorry. . . ."

I don't remember much more from that night, except Worm trying to wake me some time in the morning and then feeling my forehead and letting me sleep.

I finally woke up around five o'clock in the afternoon. Even I could tell I stank from sweat. I twisted wildly to find the clock. I saw the time and went into panic.

"Geez! I slept all day! I've got to get to the computer center—finish my program!"

"Just take it easy, Mike." It was Worm. "I don't think you'll be going anywhere for the moment."

"But—but the Mikans!" I tried to jump up and felt a puzzling weakness and dizziness. "The Mikans . . . !"

"They're safe, Mike. Relax."

"What?"

"I'm not going to the computer center today—not till you can defend yourself, anyway. Okay?" He sat down on the corner of the bed. "I want you to be there to see it when you get creamed."

I leaned back against the pillow. "You wish it, Worm," I whispered.

He smiled. "And don't think I wasn't tempted to go down there—especially after I got this." He waved a slip of paper in my face. "But it's *our* game, and we'll finish it together."

"What's 'this'?"

"A social invitation. The guy at the desk delivered it in person. He said he knew we'd never find it in the mailbox." Worm laughed soundlessly. "Dean Stanley requests that we meet with him tomorrow morning at nine 'to discuss our continued standing at Franklin.' He certainly phrased it politely. I gather that that's one of the skills one acquires from a liberal arts education, in the best Franklin tradition."

For a moment the words just swirled around in my head without taking on any meaning. Dean Stanley? Continued standing at Franklin? What had they to do with my Mikans and UNIVERSE PRIME? Then my head cleared, and I put it all together. "Probation?"

"That's what it sounds like."

"But that's ridiculous! We just invented the most detailed, elaborate, significant computer game in existence!"

"That's what I intend to tell Dean Stanley. But I'm afraid he may be less impressed with that than with rules. And I can't deny we've broken a few. I think they might have been happier if we'd dropped in on classes a little more often. It might have been a mistake to neglect that."

Worm handed me the note. It was different from the others Dean Stanley had sent; for one thing it was typed, on official Franklin stationery, and the language was stiff and formal. No more plaintive, handwritten jottings, no more cajoling. This time he meant business. The threat was veiled, but unmistakeable. I couldn't put him off any longer; this time I'd have to see him, and Worm would, too.

I struggled to get up again and felt rage when my body wouldn't obey me. Trivialities, getting in my way again! First, Dean Stanley, with his small mind and bureaucratic rules. And now, with only hours left to save the Mikans before meeting with the Dean, my body—my *body*, of all the little, insignificant things!—chose to conk out on me!

"I think you overdid it, Mike. As a matter of fact, when I saw that you weren't getting up, I caught up on a number of hours of sleep, myself. Supposing I get you some of that chemical junk they call hot chicken soup from the machine downstairs?"

"Sounds good. Maybe if that helps, we can still get in a few hours at the computer center."

Worm smiled faintly. "I was hoping you'd say that!"

"We've still got seven hours!" I tried to sit up again, but my body felt like lead.

6 The Franklin Ideal

The chemical chicken soup helped a little, but not enough. I could tell that Worm was anxious to get back to the computer center. The closer it got to closing time, the more upset he seemed at the slowness of my recovery, but he didn't pressure me. He just seemed to tighten inside and keep looking at his watch. I was equally tense.

"Well," Worm said with a sigh when it became apparent that we weren't going anywhere, "I've never heard of the computer center being declared off-limits as part of academic probation. We'll just have to suffer without football games or basketball or debating club or all those other activities we love."

I grunted and went back to sleep.

I woke up with a start the next morning to the sensation of Worm tugging at my covers. Eight-thirty! We were behind schedule already, and far beyond any chance we might have had of sneaking in a quick run-through of the next phase of our game. How could I have slept through my one chance? I hadn't even thought

of what the Dean might do to us: kick us out
of school? Bar us from the computer center? I
didn't even know what I'd say to him, how to
deal with this bureaucrat who had the power
to take away from me everything I now cared
about.

We both showered and put on fresh pairs of
jeans to make ourselves presentable. Worm even
shaved. I was still a little weak on my feet, so I
fortified myself with a bowl of cornflakes and
milk, on the theory that a little nutrition might
help me keep my head clear.

We were fifteen minutes late when we walked
into the Dean's office.

"Well, sit down." Dean Stanley looked up from
a folder he was examining. I felt as if I were
being called into the principal's office—one of
those principals who likes to act as if he's really
just a pal, except you always know that he's the
principal and you're not. The last time I had
seen him, weeks and weeks ago, Dean Stanley
had been doing his pal routine; I wondered if
he'd use it now.

"Mr. Goldman." He smiled briefly. After three
months at school, it still felt weird to be called
that. "And Mr. Evans—" He turned to Worm.
"I don't believe you and I have met before."

"That's right," said Worm.

"Hi," I murmured.

"Hi." He looked at me. "Mr. Goldman, we
seem to have been missing each other for almost
two months now."

His expression was so deadpan, I couldn't be
sure if he was being ironic or not.

"I know," I answered.

"Well, I'm glad you could both make it this morning. Because we definitely have some things to talk over."

I squirmed.

"I must confess, I've been rather lax over the past month or so. I got involved with other duties, and I just didn't realize how much time had gone by since we'd touched base. Well, from now on, I'm going to make sure that we stay in closer touch. *Much* closer touch. Agreed?"

I didn't have a choice, and I knew it. "Okay."

"Good. Now, Mr. Evans. I'm not your advisor, of course; but, under the circumstances, I thought it would be a good idea for us to talk, too."

Worm's mouth twitched. "'The circumstances.'"

"You know, you both entered this school with great promise—especially you, Mr. Goldman. Even with your outstanding achievements, however, there were those who felt that perhaps it was a mistake to admit you at so young an age. They felt you might not have the maturity and steadiness required to make full use of a college education." He smiled apologetically. "I'm sorry to say, you seem to be proving those people right."

My mouth went dry.

"You both started out the term rather well. Then, all of a sudden, things seemed to drop off. You both stopped attending most of your classes. Mr. Goldman, you now have four incompletes! and Mr. Evans, you have three—all of which are in danger of being converted to F's if something isn't done quickly. I suggest you both contact your professors immediately to find out what assignments and tests you need to make up. I was planning to contact you both this week anyway, probably separately; then last week, I heard mention of some rather unorthodox procedures at the computer center, and I discovered that you were roommates, so I thought a joint conference might be in order, to help us get to the bottom of things. And—um, Mr. Goldman, yesterday I received a rather unusual phone call from your mother."

Geez! I felt like strangling her. I could feel my face burning.

"She wanted to know what had become of you, to be sure that you hadn't been kidnapped by gypsies or God knows what. Now, ordinarily, matters of communication between students and their parents can be resolved without recourse to the university. But in your case, the school *is* prepared to take an extra measure of responsibility, because of your age. I trust that you won't make that necessary."

I swallowed. "No."

"Good." Dean Stanley leaned back. "So, all these things coming together—well, it makes me wonder what goes on here."

Why? Because some people found some things more interesting than your dumb classes? I didn't dare say it.

The Dean was talking again. "Now, look, Mr. Goldman, Mr. Evans. I know you're both in a difficult situation; being thrust into college work

and living on one's own can be a problem even
for students who are the same age as everyone
else in class. My job is to help you—and any
freshman—with problems you might be having;
I want you to feel free to talk to me. It doesn't
have to wait until things become so acute that
I can see there's a problem. *You* can call on me
any time *you* feel that there's a problem." He
paused. "How do you both feel about your experience at Franklin so far?"

What did he want? Was there some right answer that would make things less bad? I groped.
"It's okay."

Worm nodded in agreement.

"Are you fitting in socially?"

"Oh, yeah, sure."

"Any problems of any kind?"

"No, of course not."

Dean Stanley gave me a searching look. "Are
you sure? When students doing 'A' work suddenly stop attending classes and start neglecting
themselves, I think there must be some kind of
problem."

Worm and I glanced at each other. There was
an awkward silence that felt like an hour. At
last Worm opened his mouth to speak. And suddenly, I knew what he was going to say. He'd
told me yesterday, but I had been too sick to
listen. The idiot! Didn't he realize our danger?
I tried to warn him with my expression, but
Worm didn't seem to notice.

"There isn't any problem. Actually we've just
been working on—"

"Well, I guess I'd better admit it," I broke in

desperately with the only idea I could think of. "We just got a little too caught up in the school spirit. We've been spending a lot of time following the football games."

"Football?" The Dean looked dubious. Worm gave me a puzzled look.

"Well, yeah, you know how it is. First you start watching the games, then you start watching the practice sessions. I never realized how fascinating the game could be before. Finally I found I'd been spending all my time watching football. I guess we just kind of let it get away from us. We're really sorry, and we won't let it happen again."

Dean Stanley smiled out of one side of his mouth. I hoped with all my strength that that meant he sympathized, but I knew it didn't. "Mr. Goldman—the football season ended a month ago."

I felt like an idiot. "Oh—um, basketball. I didn't mean football, I meant basketball." My face felt as if it was in a furnace. I couldn't look Dean Stanley in the eyes, but I could tell he was staring at me.

There was another hour-long pause.

"As I started to say," Worm resumed, breaking the silence, "there isn't any problem. It's just that we've been working—"

I nudged Worm frantically. He stared back at me.

"We've been working on kind of a special project of our own, and we got so involved we just didn't have time for anything else."

The jerk! Here he was, a master of strategy for computer games, and he couldn't even tell what a colossal blunder he was making. I glared at him furiously.

Dean Stanley, meanwhile, showed signs of interest. He nodded his head several times to show that he was considering the explanation with due gravity. "Ah-ha. What kind of project?"

Worm smiled faintly. I knew that smile: he was building up steam to plunge full-speed ahead with a spirited discourse. My heart sank. "It's a computer game, perhaps the most elaborate ever built," he began. "It's far beyond anything that's ever been done before. What we've developed here is a model for an entire universe, in all its aspects, with extremely complex and detailed programing. It would take me hours to even begin to explain what we've accomplished in the past months. We've been working on it day and night, so I'm sure you can understand why we haven't had time for ordinary classwork. It was Michael's idea. I think we've taken computer games to a new level!" He looked so pleased with himself I could have spit.

The Dean nodded again. "That's quite impressive. Have you been consulting with Professor Kirstin on this?"

"No, we figured it out all on our own!"

Blunder number two. I stared at the floor.

"Very impressive. A whole universe?"

There was nothing left but to play it the way Worm had started, to press through with his strategy all the way. I gave it a desperate try.

"That's right," I answered, "a whole universe. We're programing star maps, planets, physics, biology, chemistry—"

"Even time travel!" Worm interjected.

The Dean raised his eyebrows. "Time travel?"

For a split second I pictured what Worm would look like with a couple of reels of computer tape jammed down his throat.

"That one's just an exercise," I broke in quickly. "But we're doing chemistry, economics, ecology, politics, psychology—it's like taking a hundred courses in everything!"

Worm chimed in. "We're learning more now than we'd ever learn in class!"

Dean Stanley smiled the same smile he had smiled when I mentioned football. We were sunk, I knew it. "Really! But no, it's not quite the same thing as taking a hundred courses in everything." He sighed. "You two are putting me in a very difficult position. I certainly don't want to discourage independent study . . ."

Then don't, I thought.

"On the contrary," he continued, "at Franklin we make an effort to provide gifted young men like yourselves with every opportunity to pursue independent projects—with the proper supervision." The axe was about to fall. "But only after you've studied the basics. We have a philosophy of education here, what we like to call the Franklin Ideal." The Dean warmed to his subject; it was obviously one of his favorite speeches. "At Franklin, we want to provide you with a broad cultural background. That's particularly true of the required freshman-year courses. We don't want to produce narrow specialists who are ignorant of everything outside their field; we want to bring out men and women who, while they are experts in one field, certainly, also have a background in the entire culture, so that they can speak to the world at large and apply their own field of expertise to the entire culture."

"But that's just what we're doing now!"

Stanley smiled again. "Yes, in a way you are."

"In a *way!*"

He held up a finger for silence and continued. "If you could have worked on this without neglecting your classes, I think we might have found a way to bend the rules and allow it. But your classes *have* suffered, to put it mildly. You're cheating yourselves of the very background you'll need to make a mature synthesis of the type you're struggling with now. You can pursue your own project any time. But these classes are only available to you now. I'm afraid I'll have to recommend that you postpone further work on this project until you've caught up with your course work and made satisfactory progress in your regular classes."

"What?!"

Worm and I both blurted out our objections at once.

"But we're almost finished!"

"If we can just finish going through it once—it will only take a day or two!"

"After all this work!"

The Dean was a little startled by our outburst.

He held up his finger again and waited until we had subsided.

"I'm sorry, but this is what I've decided is best in this case."

"But—"

"I'm giving instructions to the computer center. From now until further notice, any computer work you do must be signed by Professor Kirstin before you will be permitted to feed it into the computer." I saw a faint glimmer of hope; Dean Stanley promptly dashed it. "And I'm requesting Professor Kirstin to sign for only authorized classroom work until your other course work has returned to a satisfactory level and remained there for at least a month."

"A month!"

"That means, even if we finish all our other work tomorrow, we still can't finish our game until next term!"

"Yes, I'm aware of that. I want to be sure that you're both on a firm academic footing before we leave you open to temptation again. I know that this is disappointing now, but in the long run I think it will be best for you."

I searched frantically for other arguments. Wasn't there *any* way I could convince him of how unfair he was being? The game was in midstream, at the very climax—couldn't we get to play it all, from beginning to end, even *once?* It was all so ridiculous, for one awful minute I thought I'd start crying right in the middle of the office. Worm, meanwhile—who caused the whole thing—Worm just sat there in complete shock; if I hadn't been just as shafted myself, I would have thought it served him right.

"Idiot!" I glared at Worm as we left the office. "I *told* you not to mention the computer game!"

"You did not!"

"Well, I *signaled* you. I couldn't have been more obvious if I tried!"

"Yeah," sneered Worm. " 'Football games!' "

"At least it's better than what *you* said! If you hadn't told him about the game, he wouldn't have known to stop it!"

"And if it hadn't been for you, we might have finished it yesterday!"

It was a low blow. I didn't have anything to say. At last Worm spoke again, quietly.

"I thought I could win him over; you know, show him how much we're learning this way."

"*Were* learning," I corrected him. We were silent for a long moment. "What do we do now?"

"I don't know about you," said Worm, "but I'm going back to the room and get severely depressed."

7 Formulae M6, 7, 8

Worm's idea was the best I'd heard all day. For weeks we had lived only for UNIVERSE PRIME. Now, to have it snatched away from us . . . it was too much. And besides, we were just plain zonked. Returning to our classwork, or any such mundane consideration, was totally out of the question.

So we sat. Around noontime, Buzz knocked on the door; when we didn't answer, he opened it and stuck his head in.

"How'd the meeting go?"

I was sprawled in the armchair. Worm was slumped at his desk. Both of us looked and felt like zombies. We didn't even look up at Buzz.

"That bad, huh?"

I felt I really should give some kind of response and finally managed a grunt. Worm grimaced and gave a barely perceptible nod. It took all the energy either of us had at the moment.

"Uh, I'm sorry," Buzz fumbled. "Listen, Mike, your mother called again. She said . . ." I stared out into space. "Uh, never mind, I'll tell you later."

As he closed the door, I caught an expression on his face that indicated he thought we were crazy. I'm sure he concluded we had both finally gone off the deep end. He probably wondered what took us so long.

That was the last time either of us moved for over an hour. At last Worm broke the silence.

"Rats."

It was a fair comment.

He took in a breath and sat up. "Well, Mike, at least we got *almost* to the end."

I stared at him.

"Well, we *did.*"

I shook my head. There was no use explaining. Even Worm didn't understand.

Worm would have been satisfied just with that: to play the game through once to the end, perhaps even program a satisfyingly spectacular visual effect as the planet exploded, and then be done with it until the next time. When all was said and done, it was still the arcade-game mentality. That was never what I wanted. If playing through one arbitrary set of possibilities was all—if that was it—why bother? You might as well stay in the real universe and use the one arbitrary set of possibilities you had to work with there. What I'd loved was the chance to go back. I wanted to work through one version of reality and then go back and change it, improve it. That chance was made possible by time travel—the one function that could exist only in a computer universe. That was what made UNIVERSE PRIME different from the real universe—and better. That was what all my work had been leading up to. It was sitting there, just waiting for me in our program. And now I couldn't use it.

"Mike?" Worm passed his hand back and forth in front of my face, as if to call me back from another world.

I looked at him.

"I'm going downstairs. You want some tea or something?"

I shook my head. I barely noticed when he left.

It was some time later when Margie knocked on the door. She had to knock more than once before I really noticed it.

"Mike?" She opened the door, then gave me a funny look. "Mike, are you okay?"

"Yeah, I'm fine."

She didn't look convinced. "I heard the meeting didn't go too well. Buzz told me." She waited for me to say something; I didn't. "Mike, if there's anything—"

"Yeah, well . . ." Somehow I couldn't deal with sympathy or good wishes just then. I waved the subject away. "What can I do for you?"

She held out some computer papers. "This was in your box at the computer center. I thought you might need it."

"My print-out?" I sat up straight. "Margie, thanks!"

I reached for the papers.

"Mike, before you get all excited, it looks like you forgot to close the file in your program, so it's just printing the same program over and over."

I looked at the print-out. She was right. I'd been careless that last night. As a result, the computer was reading and rereading all available issues of *The Weekly Science Review*, and was almost certainly reading them still, even though the print-out had been stopped after about the ninetieth repetition. It all looked fairly straightforward, even unsurprising, except for the endless repeats.

And then I realized *what* it was repeating.

In my hands was a list of all available data on the behavior of subatomic particles, gathered from the *Review* from January 3, 1973, to the present—data that fit with prevailing theories and data that was still questioned and unexplained. Every bit of data there was, hundreds and hundreds of lines, had been tested out against my time-travel formulae. And at the bottom of each list, before the print-out started all over again, was the single line:

DATA THAT CONFLICT WITH
FORMULAE M6, 7, 8: NONE.

It took a minute for the information to sink in. When it did, my eyes popped.

"Mike . . . ? Is something wrong?"

I must have looked pretty wild. I tried to calm myself. "No—no, nothing's wrong at all!"

Margie looked at me uncertainly.

"It's okay, really," I told her. I smiled crazily.

"I've just got to work something out. Thanks a lot!"

My mind was racing as I looked over the print-out. Already I was forgetting that she was even there. The next time I looked up, she was gone.

I read over the print-out again. There was no mistake. Current theory still left sizeable chunks of data inadequately explained, chunks like the data in the *Review* article I'd started from, and chunks in other articles I hadn't even read or thought about. Yet my formulae—formulae I'd invented almost as a lark—accounted for all of them!

My head swam. I'd invented these formulae only as part of a make-believe universe; I'd never dreamed they'd be anything else. But I *had* used real-universe data as my starting point. And here was a print-out telling me that my time-travel formulae just might apply to the real world as well.

I tore through the papers on my desk. Piles tumbled and intermixed and landed on the floor, but I didn't care. In five minutes I'd found it: the *Review* article that had inspired my formulae, the one about Professor Terence Miller in Ohio and his peculiar observations. I read it through again—really read it for the first time—and suddenly it didn't seem quite so far-fetched.

Time travel in the real universe? Well, I wasn't prepared to go quite that far. But, at least in some mathematical sense, my formulae seemed to work. *They actually worked.* And suddenly I had a whole new world to explore.

It wasn't definite, of course. It was anything but definite. I'd need lots more data to really check it out: data gathered under special conditions like the ones Miller was experimenting with in Ohio. But that could be checked. And I was going to check it. Now.

I grabbed my overnight bag and packed my notebooks and computer programs. Then I tore a few pages off the latest program, scrawled "Ohio" across the top, and left it on Worm's bed as a clue: it was the least I could do for him— and the most I had time for.

I stopped at the bank and withdrew a hundred fifty dollars of the money that was intended for part of next term's tuition and school expenses, but this was more important. I caught a local bus to the depot and bought a ticket.

Minutes later, I was on a bus—bound for Ohio and Professor Terence Miller.

8 Ohio

SUBATOMIC PARTICLES IN TIME TRAVEL?

Professor Terence Miller, of the University of Ohio, reports some highly suggestive preliminary findings in his tracking of subatomic particles during the decay of a neutron. According to Miller's report, under certain conditions, a subatomic particle may appear to occupy two different positions at the same moment; at other moments, the same particle seems to disappear entirely. Further testing is underway, but Miller theorizes that, if his results so far are reliable, the particle in question may actually be engaged in time travel for periods of a microsecond or so—disappearing from one moment to meet itself in another moment.

That was it: one paragraph, followed by a thin listing of sample data. That was the story in *The Weekly Science Review* that had started it all. I read it and reread it as the bus continued on its way.

I could hardly believe what I was doing. Here I was, a kid who under normal circumstances could just about keep track of his own room number, on a bus on my own, trying to find my way to God-Knows-Where, Ohio. And that was the *least* incredible part about it. I laughed.

That morning I had felt absolutely hopeless. Now I had a new sense of possibility. There was hope even for UNIVERSE PRIME. After all, if I could show that it had given rise to something important that applied to the real world, even Dean Stanley couldn't stop us from playing. And if worse came to worst—if it was all a tremendous mistake—at the very least, I'd stumbled on a way to keep up the game and take steps to save the Mikans before next term. After all, the computer was still reading *The Weekly Science Review*, and would continue reading it and transferring the relevant information to Mikan data banks, until someone told it to stop. If certain concepts could find their way into one of the *Review*'s upcoming issues—by way of a follow-up to certain peculiar observations in Ohio—well, it would be almost like programing my next move, without going near the computer center!

Those were the possibilities for our game. There were possibilities for the *real* universe that I didn't even allow myself to think about.

That evening, from a rest stop, I called my room long distance. I recognized the voice.

"Hi, Buzz!"

"Mike? Where the heck are you?"

"It's hard to say, exactly. Just tell Worm to keep an eye on Mikan data banks."

There was a long pause. "Mikan data banks."

"Right. Margie can check it out for him at

the computer center. He'll know what it means.'

"Wonderful. You know, your mother's half-crazy worrying about you."

"Tell her I'm okay, would you?"

"*You* tell her!" Buzz exploded. "*You* call her What do you think this is, your personal answering service? She's calling every hour on the hour driving *me* crazy. She wants to know when you're coming home for Christmas vacation."

"Christmas vacation?"

"It starts in two days, remember?"

"Oh."

" 'Oh.' She says if you don't show up soon, she's sending a private detective after you."

"Well, I tend to doubt that; but I expect to be home, anyway." The bus driver flashed his lights. "Listen, Buzz, I've got to go. Just tell Worm—"

"Yeah, I know—the Mikan data banks."

"Right. Take care!"

I figured I could afford to give Worm that extra clue—it was only fair. And besides, knowing Worm, he might not get it, anyway.

I still had a few more hours to sit on the bus. Rereading the *Review* article and its list of data got my creative juices flowing. I began to play around with my formulae, experimenting with ways of refining them further. I had originally written them as three linked equations; but I now saw that with just a slight twist to the first equation, the third seemed to become superfluous. I could get exactly the same results from the two equations as I would have gotten before from all three. I eliminated the third equation accordingly and chalked up two points for economy.

I finally got off at a little town called Greenville, where I'd get my connecting bus the next day. The place apparently had a few factories to its credit and not much else. It wasn't exactly crawling with tourists, and I was the only passenger to get off the bus at eleven o'clock at night.

There was a hotel across the street from where the bus let me off—a rundown five-story building that had the temerity to call itself The Plaza. Whatever else you could say about it, and there was plenty, it had three advantages: it was there, it had vacancies, and it was cheap. Those were hard facts to argue with. I don't know what I would have done if it hadn't been there.

When I opened the door, a bell rang on top, waking up the clerk who was snoozing behind the desk. He focused on me slowly and massaged his grizzled cheeks to get himself more awake.

"I'd like a room," I said.

"For yourself?"

The question seemed so unnecessary that I was tempted to deadpan, "No, it's for my pet canary," or something to that effect. But this was the only hotel around as far as I knew, so I just said, "Yes."

He stared at me a long time, making me very uncomfortable and kind of angry. If it took him this long to process routine information, however could he react when he faced a *real* problem?

At last he spoke. "What are you doing here?"

"Just visiting."

"You one of those runaways?"

Geez. So *that's* what was going through his mind.

"No. I'm not."

"How do I know?"

I tried to sound patient and reasonable. "Because kids run from here to New York, not the other way around Now may I have a room please?"

I don't think he really bought that. I'd have been surprised if he had But I guess he didn't feel like arguing.

"You got money?"

"Sure."

He reached for a key and placed it on the desk, his hand still covering it. "Ten dollars. In advance."

I gave him the money. He released the key "Room 508. The stairs are in back."

He leaned his chair back up against the wall and nodded—the fastest snooze in the West. I wondered if he'd even remember me in the morning. He cocked open an eye. "Don't forget to sign the book."

I signed the register and followed the hallway to a dimly lit staircase. The stairs were covered with a worn carpet that may once have been red. Five flights was a long way to climb

I felt kind of a vague anxiety when I opened the door and surveyed the room: cracked paint and crumbling plaster on the walls, an old iron bed with a lumpy mattress, a rickety dresser, and a chair. It wasn't even as nice as the older dorms on campus Not that I usually cared about such things. I guess the reaction was just sort of a vestige of my middle-class upbringing. And it was cold. That was the worst part. Since the blankets seemed pretty thin, I'd have to sleep in my clothes.

It suddenly hit me: this was the first room that was totally mine that I'd ever had, free from prying parents pounding on the door demanding to know why I wasn't out doing something else, free from roommates sharing the same space, free from authorities. Mine. No one here would even know who I was. They could see that I was young, certainly, and bright and strange. But I doubted very much whether anyone would be able to tell that I was a genius. Without a school setting to define me that way, the term suddenly lost a good part of its meaning. It was a strange feeling, not having to play that part for a few hours. It left me feeling a little insecure, but also strangely relieved. If there'd only been a little more heat, it would have been perfect.

I hesitated a moment, then picked up the phone on the night table. It rang a few times; then I recognized a sleepy voice answering at the other end.

"Yeah?"

"This room has no heat."

"We provide heat until eight o'clock. That's the law."

"It doesn't feel as if there was any heat here any time at all today."

"Well, you just checked in. What do you expect, that we'd heat it all day just for you?"

"Well, could I at least have an extra—"

He hung up. Jerk. And a jerky law, too. if that really was the law.

Forget it, I told myself. Tomorrow I'd have more important things to deal with. Much more important.

I took off my shoes, climbed into bed fully clothed, bundled up in my coat and the blankets—and made a mental note to program liberal heating laws for the WORM FARM at my next opportunity.

9 Crucial Tests

I reached the University of Ohio late the follow
ing afternoon. It was a big, sprawling campus,
easy to get lost in. Already it was emptying out
for Christmas vacation. I asked directions and
scrambled through a maze of unfamiliar build-
ings until at last I found Professor Miller's office.

It was small and dark and almost as messy as
my dorm room, with books and notepads bal-
anced in precarious piles on the desk top. A man
who looked as if he couldn't be more than twenty
stood behind the desk packing a few things into
a briefcase and getting ready to go. I was sure
he was too young to be the professor.

"Excuse me, I'm looking for Professor Miller."

"I'm Professor Miller." He spoke with a deep
voice and had a surprising suavity and charm
about him—like the movie stars from about
twenty years ago. All in all, he was not quite
what I expected.

I must have been staring at him, because he
waited a minute and then said, "Yes?"

"Did you skip a few years or something?" I
blurted out and immediately felt like a nerd. I

was not making a dynamic first impression. He would think I was just some dumb kid in a winter coat, clutching an overnight bag.

Miller half-smiled in amusement. "I'm a little older than I look. Can I help you?"

"Uh, yeah. My name is Michael Goldman, and I saw an item about your research in *The Weekly Science Review.*" Somehow my statement sounded like a question.

"And you're interested in the time-travel hypothesis. Of course, these are just preliminary findings. They might be explainable by some kind of time travel, as the magazine suggests, or they might be caused by interference from some other particle we haven't isolated yet or a hundred other possible reasons."

"Which do *you* think it is?"

Miller gave a faint, conspiratorial smile, and his voice lowered with just a hint of excitement. "Strictly off the record . . . I think it's the time travel!"

"Would these formulae conform with the rest of your data?" I picked out a pen and notepad from my overnight bag and scribbled my revised time-travel formulae from UNIVERSE PRIME.

Miller's expression turned to shock, then to pondering, as he looked over what I'd written. "Where did you get this?"

"I made it up. Does it fit with your other data?"

"It might. It might." He grabbed his coat and finished stuffing his papers into his briefcase. "Why don't you come along with me?"

He ushered me out of his office and locked the door. I hurried to keep up with him as he rushed down the corridors.

"Where are we going?"

"I'm sorry. Sometimes when I get excited, I just expect people to know what I'm thinking."

"Oh. Well, where *are* we going?"

"To the computer room to try this out."

"The formulae aren't complicated. Why don't we just try a few values by hand first?"

Miller smiled sheepishly. "I was always terrible at algebra."

"What?"

"I have a tendency to keep making careless errors in the simplest parts of the calculation Of course, over the years I've had to develop a certain competency at it; but when there's a choice, I still feel more secure doing it by machine. That way I know I won't be wrecking my computations with a simple arithmetic error."

Miller again studied the scrap of paper on which I'd written my formulae, and almost bumped into a water fountain He didn't notice his near collision

"What did you say your name was?"

"Michael."

"Michael, how did you happen to make up these formulae?"

I told him the whole story of our computer game and our science fiction time-travel function that was to help differentiate UNIVERSE

PRIME from the real universe. And I told him about Dean Stanley's edict and our exile from the computer center.

Miller laughed. "Well, you may have something that'll show that dean of yours!"

I laughed, too. I liked Miller; I felt I could understand him.

Everyone in the computer room recognized Professor Miller. Some of the students seemed to look at him with a kind of awe and were obviously puzzled by the sight of a shrimp tagging behind him. It was understood that this was a man of importance.

Miller logged on and entered my formulae and then punched up a list of some of his most recent data—data that derived from the special cases that would provide my formulae with their first real test. He pushed a few more keys, instructing the computer to plug the data into my formulae. The screen paused a moment, then displayed the answers.

Miller and I exchanged looks. He punched up a second sampling of data, and a third. Again we studied the display. The message was clear.

"Revolutionary . . . !" Miller murmured. "Do you know how long we've been working, trying to find a formula that will fit this data?" He gazed at me in sheer amazement. "Revolutionary . . ."

I tried to phrase it as carefully as possible. "Then . . . I guess you could say, at least in some mathematical sense, that the formulae apply."

Miller grinned broadly. "Yes. I think you could say that."

My head was spinning. I tried to keep my thoughts from flying out in all directions. "So, again, in this same mathematical sense, that might mean—"

"Michael—" He cut me off. "You keep saying 'in some mathematical sense,' as if that saved it from being entirely real, as if you can't quite accept it yet yourself."

I scarcely breathed. "Should I?"

"Well . . . to my way of thinking, if it's true in a mathematical sense, then it's true—period!"

"You mean, in other words—"

"In other words"—Miller's eyes shone with a quiet intensity—"in other words, Michael, I think you may have just demonstrated the existence of time travel!"

My mouth hung open. My eyes felt as if they were open so wide I couldn't have closed them if I wanted to. Miller was right, of course. It had been under my nose all along—it had even been my secret, unacknowledged dream when I first imagined a UNIVERSE PRIME—but somehow I couldn't quite believe it. Not until now. My heart pounded, and all at once the excitement spilled through for both of us.

Miller saw my expression and laughed. "Michael, of course we'll have to do further testing— see if these formulae can predict results as well as explain them. But, if things work out the way I think they will, you may have just secured the Nobel Prize for both of us!"

I tried to seem nonchalant, but inside I was bubbling. "Really?"

"Really! You know, people have been saying for years that I'll probably be the youngest scientist in history to win the Nobel Prize, though don't tell anybody I said so. But can you imagine their reaction if you and I win it *together?* How old *are* you, if you don't mind my asking?"

"Thirteen." I was so excited that my voice squeaked.

Miller laughed. "Well, *that* should get some notice!" I liked his reaction. Most people made me feel like either a freak or some dumb kid who couldn't *really* be as bright as he seemed. Miller made me feel like a colleague.

The professor looked out toward the window. For a moment, his mind seemed far away. "Michael," he said at last, "do you know what this means? This may be applicable to more than subatomic particles. With these formulae and the proper technological development, it may one day be possible for *persons* to travel in time, perhaps even in the not so distant future! Of course that's only speculation at this point, but can you imagine the possibilities?"

I imagined. I could see the possibilities for history, science, exploration, novel vacations. I imagined some more—and came down off my cloud.

"Professor Miller?"

"Call me Terry."

"Terry, could we take some time to program UNIVERSE PRIME into the computer and then run through the consequences if people discover how to travel in time?"

"I thought that was already known in UNI-VERSE PRIME."

"Not by people, just by Worm and me. In the game we're kind of like . . . guiding spirits." I said the last phrase with some embarrassment.

"What will happen if people learn how to travel in time? Of course, you realize that your universe is just a model, a game. It can suggest some possibilities, but it can never tell us exactly what will happen for sure."

"I invented the thing. Don't you think I know that?"

"M'm sorry. Sure, let's do it. I'd like to see this game. Harold!" He called over a youngish man who seemed to be in charge of the computers. "See if you can get me a hookup to the computer at Franklin College in New York."

Harold made the connection, and I supplied my account number and job code. Terry scanned the video screen as the information came in; he was dazzled by the detail of my program. "Unbelievable!" he would say in a soft voice from time to time. "I've never seen anything quite like this! And this is the first computer game you've invented? It's really an admirable job!"

In minutes, the program was ready. My toes tingled. At last I could finish the game with the move I'd been waiting for! I felt a twinge of guilt that Worm was not there to share the moment, especially after he had restrained himself the day I got sick. But more than the game was at stake now. I had to know the answer to the question I had posed.

I advanced the time to approximately the present day and typed in the information that scientists on PLANET MIKO had discovered the time travel formulae. Then I let time on PLANET MIKO go ahead at the rate of ten years of MIKO time for one minute of our time.

A peculiar thing happened. In less than ten minutes the readings for all life forms, cities, human inventions, etc., dropped to zero—and remained that way even when we scanned the time frame backwards to the beginning of the planet.

"What happened?" asked Terry.

"I'm not sure," I admitted. "Let's try it again."

We checked over the program and ran it through again—with the same results.

I felt an incredible anxiety and frustration. The results were clearly impossible. Here I was, showing my creation for the first time to someone who could really appreciate it. And the program chose now of all times to reveal some new bugs in it! I felt like kicking the computer to make it work. "It's very odd," was all I could say. "Nothing like this has ever happened before."

Terry frowned in concentration. "According to this, not only have all life forms been destroyed, but now they never even existed."

"I noticed that." Despite myself, a tinge of sarcasm crept into my voice. I thought a minute and sat up straight in my chair. Might it be possible, after all? "Maybe—maybe it's not a mistake! If we're allowing the Mikans to travel in time, the past and the future might be changed as a result. Say we repeat the same procedure we just did, and at the same time pick out a few specific points in time and monitor them. You know, a specific moment in the past, like twelve noon, January One, One Billion B.C., and a specific moment in the future—and see if the readings for those moments change as the present progresses."

Terry nodded. "I see your point. Yes, let's do it."

We programed the new instructions and ran through the procedure again. My neck and shoulders ached as I concentrated on the readings.

For a time, the present seemed to enjoy a remarkable renaissance. New funds of energy and vital resources were discovered, leading to renewed industrialization, productivity, and even a greatly improved quality of life. This was accompanied, amazingly enough, by a decrease in pollution to levels it had not enjoyed since the previous century. Other, quite different changes were taking place in the other moments we were monitoring. In our moment in 50,000 A.D., pollution was increasing to highly toxic levels. And in our moment in 1 billion B.C., resources were fast disappearing: clean air and water, minerals, forests, algae. When the resources reached a critically low level, all readings suddenly dipped to zero across the board—at all moments in time.

Terry and I stared at the readout. I felt a moment of vindication. My program *had* worked, after all! Then I thought about it and wished it hadn't, that it had all been a mistake. I had dreamed up time travel as a second chance for survival; instead, it was just one more means of destruction.

"I see." said Terry softly.

"Yeah. They're transporting all their pollution and poisons to the future and then going back and raiding the past for its resources. When resources in the present are nearly used up, they just organize a little expedition to the past and pick up whatever they need. Except, when they reach far enough back into the past, the conditions needed to support life are very fragile. If they take enough resources from that time, life just can't develop. And once that happens, then it all just never was."

Terry nodded. "That does seem to be the most reasonable explanation of the readings."

I felt a sudden pang of anxiety. "Excuse me a minute." I ran out into the hallway.

"Where are you going?"

"I've just got to make a phone call."

I reached a pay phone, inserted a dime, and dialed my room in Franklin. Terry waited a few yards away.

"Two dollars and five cents for the first three minutes, please," said the operator. I could hear the phone ringing at the other end as I fumbled in my pocket—and fished out fifteen cents.

"Hello?" It was Worm's voice.

"Worm!"

"Just a minute, please," said the operator "Please deposit two dollars and five cents."

Cretins at the phone company! All they care about is their rules and their two dollars and five cents. I fished again in my pocket and dropped out my wallet onto the floor. I tried to pick it up but couldn't reach it without dropping the receiver. "Terry, do you have some change?"

"That's all right, operator." It was Worm's voice again. "I'll accept the charges."

"You'll accept the charges?" asked the operator, brilliantly.

"Yes, reverse the charges."

"Thanks, Worm."

"That's okay. You can pay it when we get the bill. I've been waiting for your call."

"You have?"

"Sure. I got the hint from your message and that program you left me. If the computer is still reading *The Weekly Science Review*, then all you have to do is somehow get something published there and it goes straight into UNIVERSE PRIME. That's your game plan, right?"

"Well, it occurred to me."

"I'll bet it did. So I'm playing that way, too. I got Margie to run off the few calculations for me—"

"Worm, listen—I'm in Ohio. The time-travel formulae fit Professor Miller's data—"

"I know. I sent them off in a letter to *The Weekly Science Review*."

"You *what?*"

"Giving you full credit, of course."

"Worm—Worm, we ran through on the computer what would happen if scientists learned those formulae—"

"I know—so did I."

"Then—then you know what it *means?*"

"Yes. It means I won. Isn't it beautiful?"

"*Worm!* You *idiot!*"

"Mike, I didn't think you'd be such a sore loser I happen to think it's rather elegant, myself. No messy nuclear explosion, no slow deaths from pollution or famine. Everything just neatly cancelled, in one stroke! All life simply ceases to be! A victory for the WORM! Isn't that elegant?"

"Worm, have you gone crazy?"

Worm laughed. "Why, what do you mean?"

I groped for some way to get through to him. "Do you *hear* what you're *saying?*"

"Hey, calm down Mike. It's not as though it were all really gonna' happen."

"Isn't it?"

"Of course not!"

"Did you actually send the letter?"

"Sure—that's how we're playing it now."

"*Ugh!*"

"Mike, get a hold of yourself. We're talking about UNIVERSE PRIME, not the real world!"

I tried to control myself. My voice trembled. "*Think* a minute, you idiot—"

"Hey, now—"

"*Just listen to me!* My formulae fit Miller's observations, right?"

"Well, sure, superficially—"

"Not just superficially! We've gone over a lot of the data, and there's a pretty good chance that those formulae or something very similar just might be right."

"Really? So . . . ?"

"*So*, those formulae were the main thing that made UNIVERSE PRIME physically different. And if those formulae do turn out to be right after all, then for all practical purposes UNIVERSE PRIME *is* the real world! *So*, what you have just done, brainchild, is—"

"*Ohhh . . . !*" Worm let out a low groan, followed by a long silence. I had finally gotten through to him.

"Worm—are you still there?"

When his voice came back on the line, it sounded small and scared.

"For the time being."

10 A Man of Science

It was like a nightmare. I was still playing the same game, with the same objective. But it wasn't set in a make-believe universe anymore, and writing some clever computer program couldn't help me. It was in the real world now, and I was playing for keeps.

Terry was waiting for me at the end of the hallway.

"What did he do?" he asked.

I told him.

Terry knitted his eyebrows together. "Oh, no! You mean he stole the formulae?"

"What do you mean?"

"Well, as I understand it, those particular formulae were yours, not his. Right?"

"Well, yeah, right. But he was just trying to win the game. I'm sure he didn't mean to steal anything. But that's hardly the point, Terry. If those formulae are published—"

"Well, clearly, we can't allow him to publish.

I didn't quite follow Terry's line of thought

but I was glad that at least we were on firm ground again. "Sure, but the letter's already in the mail. How can we stop it?"

Terry grimaced. It was the same expression he had used repeatedly in the past few hours. After a few moments he spoke. "I know Logan, the editor at *The Weekly Science Review*. I'll call him in the morning and explain that Worm, in the excitement of the moment, was making unauthorized use of another student's ideas and that the research in question is not ready for publication. I've spoken with the student, who happens to be a freshman; while he's undoubtedly precocious and his formulae do seem to fit the limited data presented in the article, there is serious doubt that they can be reconciled with a more complete listing of my data, which I will soon publish."

"I see."

"Do you think Worm can be persuaded to tell them the same thing and ask them to withdraw his letter from publication?"

"I'm sure he can!"

"Well, then, I think Logan will respect that."

"Are you sure?"

Terry smiled. "You can't be *sure* of anything. Who knows? He might smell a scoop and decide to throw journalistic and scientific ethics out the window. But I don't think so. Logan edits a respectable magazine—albeit at times a little sensational. I think he'll abide by the researcher's right to decide when he's ready to publish. All we

can do now is call back Worm and then see how
Logan reacts in the morning."

It made sense. But it was frustrating to have
to wait so long without doing more.

"*Meanwhile*   " Terry interrupted my
thoughts.

"Geez, I almost forgot! Meanwhile I've got to
talk to Worm, before he leaves or something!
You got some change?"

Terry fished into his pocket and drew out a
handful of quarters and dimes.

"Thanks!"

I grabbed a handful and dialed Worm. The
phone kept ringing, but Worm didn't answer
I felt a panic creeping up on me, along with
an empty feeling in the pit of my stomach. Had
we just blown everything while I'd stood there
talking with Terry? I started counting the rings.
I didn't know how many times the phone had
rung before I started counting, but I began with
number one. I once read that you should allow
ten rings before hanging up; I'd never bothered
waiting that long before, but now I let it keep
ringing. On the ninth ring, someone picked up.

"Yeah?" The voice sounded half dead.

"Worm! Why didn't you answer?"

"I didn't know it was you. I didn't feel like
talking to anyone."

"Listen, we've got an idea."

I told Worm our plan. He listened quietly

"So," he said at last. "It's not all over. Of
course, I should have thought of that, it's so simple. Then there's still a chance."

His voice sounded strange, not quite relieved, more as if he were almost dreading the chance to undo what he'd done. I could guess what he was going through. Somehow, I too had felt more comfortable when I thought things were hopeless than when I suddenly had a hope—and had to deal with the terrible anxiety of waiting hours or days to see whether or not things would work out. In a funny way, it would have been a relief just to accept the inevitability of doomsday.

"Sure—sure, I'll do it," Worm was saying. "I'll call first thing in the morning."

"Good."

"Mike, are you coming back now? Christmas vacation starts tomorrow, you know."

I'd forgotten all about it. "I don't know yet. I'll have to see."

"Okay." Worm hesitated a moment. "Mike? I really won, right?"

"What?" I didn't want to hear this.

"The UNIVERSE PRIME game. I won, right?"

I could feel a rage growing within me. I felt like screaming into the telephone or perhaps throttling it with my bare hands. I didn't say anything.

"I mean, as far as our computers are concerned the world is destroyed. Just 'cause we're changing things now, I mean . . ."

I controlled myself. "Yeah. You won." Somehow it felt harder to concede the defeat than to accept doomsday for the real world. But it was only fair.

I hung up and turned to Terry. "He'll do it."

Terry let out his breath and smiled. "Well, that's one obstacle down. It's really the least he can do. That kid had no business sending off your formulae. It was totally irresponsible."

I wasn't feeling on the friendliest terms with Worm myself at that moment, but it irked me to hear someone else talk about him that way. "Terry . . ."

"I know, he's your friend. But it's still true." I didn't say anything. "All right, I'm sorry. I won't say any more."

"Okay."

I suddenly felt tired and hungry. The computer center was closing up. We had to rush back into the room to pick up our coats and belongings. I had no idea where I'd go next. I must have looked a little lost.

Terry had seemed far away in thought somewhere, but he suddenly came to and looked at me. "Mike, where are you staying?"

"I don't know. I came straight from Greenville this morning."

Terry paused a moment to consider, then shrugged.

"We've got a couch in the living room. It's a little lumpy, but you can sleep on it."

"Thanks. Thanks a lot. I'm sure it's better than where I slept last night."

Terry led the way to his car. It was only about ten minutes to his house. Somehow getting out into the cold and driving in the darkness seemed to dispell the gloom that had settled on me since

I had run the program through the computer that afternoon. Once we were out of the computer center, it seemed as if it all had never happened. We spent the whole drive talking excitedly about the applications of my formulae to Terry's data and the theoretical implications they led to.

We pulled into the driveway of a medium-sized stone house. Lights were burning in the living room and kitchen

A slim, well-dressed lady in her fifties met us at the door. "Terry, you're so late again; the dinner's all dried out—"

"Mom, this is Michael Goldman." Terry interrupted.

The lady seemed to notice me for the first time "Oh, I'm sorry, I didn't see you. How nice to meet you, Michael."

She gave Terry a puzzled look.

"Hi," I managed.

Terry put on his most charming manner. "Michael has generously consented to share the next Nobel Prize with me."

"Oh, really?" She smiled. "Well, that's Terry Even when he was a boy, he always shared."

"Mom.   ."

"Just teasing."

"Seriously, Mom, Michael has been discussing some fascinating ideas with me, which may have some very interesting implications for my work."

"Really!" She turned to me. "That's very interesting. Do you know Terry was written up in *The Weekly Science Review?* This one was just a little notice, but there will be much more soon."

"I know." My stomach gave a loud growl.

"Well, Michael, would you like to stay to dinner?"

"Thank you."

"Mom, Michael just got in from out of town, so I've already invited him to dinner—and to sleep over."

"Oh. Well, of course, Michael, you're welcome." She lowered her voice, though I don't know why, since obviously I could hear her just as well as Terry could. "Terry, it would have been helpful if you'd thought to call in advance. That way I could have prepared a little more for dinner, and . . ." She turned to me again. "Terry has so much on his mind, he just never thinks of these things."

"Oh. Well, if it's any trouble—"

"No, no, no trouble. You two make yourselves at home, and I'll see what I can do to freshen up dinner."

She disappeared into the kitchen, and Terry and I sat down on the couch. It *was* lumpy and ornate. We were quiet for a moment.

"I'm just so busy all the time, I never got around to moving out," Terry explained. "I hate moving. Besides, I never have time for cooking or doing the laundry or whatever, so living at home I get all that as kind of a 'fringe benefit.'" He gave a short laugh.

"Oh."

There was another silence. Terry. It even sounded like a kid's name.

"Terry, do you mind if I ask you how old you are?"

"Thirty-one." He colored slightly.

"Oh." I nodded. "Just curious."

We were silent again. After a while, I could hear Terry's mother bustling around in the kitchen. She came back in and announced dinner.

The food was better than anything I'd had in weeks, even if it was a little dried out. I could feel Mrs. Miller furtively staring at me as I gobbled down my portion in five minutes flat. I hadn't eaten all day, but it probably looked as if I'd been starving a whole year.

"I'm sorry I don't have any more pot roast to offer you," said Mrs. Miller. "I usually only cook for two. But I have some leftover chicken I could heat up. It will only take a minute."

"Oh, that's okay," I mumbled as I heaped the last shreds of meat onto my fork. "This is fine."

"Are you sure? I'll put up the chicken just in case."

"No, really." I was still hungry, but I didn't want her doing anything more for me. She was already getting up from the table. "I can eat it cold."

"Not in my house, you can't." She lifted a casserole of chicken out of the refrigerator and brought it to the oven.

It was already getting late, and I must have looked pretty dead, because right after dinner Mrs. Miller brought out some sheets and a blanket and made up the couch for me. I went straight to bed, but for a long time I couldn't sleep. Driving in the car with Terry, or sitting across the dinner table with Terry and his mother, I had thought occasionally of our doomsday problem, but it had still seemed unreal; it was just too big, too fantastic, too remote. I just couldn't feel it. Now, lying alone in the darkness, I felt a vague anxiety. Why? Oh yes, the formulae. They were out there in a letter somewhere, traveling across the country at this very minute, still not really definitely stopped. What if Logan decided to publish after all? What if the letter fell into the wrong hands? There were a thousand other "what if's" that could bring the formulae to light and start a reaction leading inexorably to the end of life on this planet. And all because of me. I wished I could just push a button on some giant computer and erase this whole game, start it all over. But I couldn't.

I finally fell asleep; I don't know how late it was, but the last time I remember looking at the clock, it was about four o'clock in the morning.

I turned my head and woke up to a crack of sunlight through the window hitting me right in the eye. I focused on the clock—eleven o'clock!—and sat up in a panic.

"Well, good morning!" called Mrs. Miller robustly. I had a feeling that this was her subtle way of remarking on my slothfully late arousal.

"Good morning. Where's Terry?"

"He's at the laboratory and has been since early this morning. Can't wait all day for sleepyheads!"

I dashed into the bathroom and changed into my clothes. I'm sure I lost caste with Mrs. Miller for not bothering to shower.

"Which way's the laboratory?"

"Why, it's at the university, straight down the road. But he can't be disturbed there!"

"I'll just take a walk then."

"Don't you want breakfast?"

"No thanks!" I pulled on my coat and hurried out the door.

It took me about an hour to walk back to the university. The campus was nearly dead, everyone gone for Christmas vacation. I found the building I'd been in the previous night and asked a guard for directions, then made my way to Terry's laboratory.

Block letters read "AUTHORIZED PERSONNEL ONLY" on a locked door. I knocked, but the door was so heavy, I doubted anyone on the other side could hear. I pounded, setting up the biggest racket I could, for what seemed like five minutes. Finally someone threw open the door from inside.

It was Terry. He seemed ready to explode in irritation at being interrupted in his experiments, but then he saw who it was and burst into a happy, excited smile. "Mike! Come on in!"

"Did you—"

"Yes, yes," he said quickly. "I called Logan first thing this morning, and it's okay. The letter won't run, no problem. Come in!" he repeated.

I entered. Filling the laboratory was a tremendous piece of metallic equipment. "This is a linear accelerator," said Terry proudly. "Ever see one of these babies before?" I hadn't. "And this is my assistant, Jim Blake. Michael Goldman."

A tall, skinny grad student stepped out from a corner and extended his hand, beaming at me. "So! You're the young man!"

I had no idea how to answer that one. "Hi," I said.

"Mike—" Terry was off at a fast clip. "Mike, we've been testing out your formulae for predictive value. I think there may have to be a few minor modifications, but all in all—it works! It works!" I thought he was going to jump into the air. "Mike, we're very excited about this here. It's definitely Nobel Prize material."

I stammered. "I thought—I thought we—"

"The computer program?"

I nodded dumbly.

"Don't take that too seriously, Mike."

"But—"

Terry turned to his assistant. "Why don't you take a little break, Jim? And bring me some coffee from the machine when you come back?"

"Sure," said Jim.

"Mike, you want anything?" Terry asked, as an after thought.

"No."

Terry shrugged, pulled up a stool, and offered me the one opposite. Jim left, and I sat down facing Terry.

"What do you think you're doing?"

Terry smiled. "Mike, calm down a minute."

"I'm calm. I asked you what you think you're doing."

"Getting us both the Nobel Prize. What do you think *you're* doing?"

"I'm . . ." It sounded too absurd to complete.

"Saving the world?"

I didn't answer.

"Mike, the work you've done is . . . extraordinary. There's no other word, extraordinary. But I think you're putting a little too much emphasis on this computer game of yours, taking it too literally. This hypothesis that your program comes up with—that if we get time travel, we'll send our pollution into the future and use up the resources from the past, until life can't develop—is a very clever premise. It's wonderful, the way it extrapolates from our present behavior, of doing almost exactly that—depleting the nonrenewable resources of the past, spewing out poisons that will accumulate and persist long into the future and thereby endangering life on the planet. The way your program develops the parallel has all the makings of excellent science fiction. That might be one fantastic way to use that program: get together with a good sci-fi writer, spin out a few hypotheses. . . ."

My breaths came short, my face burned, I felt as if I were choking. I tried to control myself. "Don't do that, Terry. Don't treat me like a kid. You think it's bull, then come out and say it."

Terry drew a breath. He seemed to be choosing his words very carefully. "I think . . . you're taking it too seriously. You've gotten very involved in this computer game, and now you're still playing it."

"It's not a game now! Don't you see? If the time travel function is correct, then UNIVERSE PRIME and the real world are the same thing!"

"No, Mike, I'm sorry. I can't accept that. No computer program, no matter how sophisticated, is 'the same as' the real world. It's a more or less accurate model, that's all. The physical laws of your model may be very close to the laws of the physical universe as we now understand them. (Which isn't to say that that understanding won't change tomorrow.) But your program's hypothesis is based on what people will do with those physical laws. Can the programed psychological profiles of one thousand imagined citizens really hope to duplicate the complex, unknown variables of the population of even a small town? Your game's hypothesis is one possibility, one bad possibility. *Any* scientific discovery can be used for good or bad. But a scientist can't concern himself with that: it's up to the people how they use it—"

"But you *can* concern yourself!"

"Mike, it's not as if we could just stop progress. If we don't publish this, sooner or later someone else will! They've all got the same research data to play with."

"But you said yourself that the data would never suggest this approach! They say they had all the data to suggest the Theory of Relativity fifty years before Einstein. But until Einstein, no one thought to look at things the way he did!"

"So now you're Einstein?" It was the obvious response, and I knew I was setting myself up for it, but I was too upset to worry about modesty. "Even if it does take fifty years, someone else will still come up with it."

"Maybe people will know how to use technology better by then."

"Do you really believe that?"

"Maybe. I don't know. Maybe." I was getting mired in details; I had to get back to the basics. "Look, do you admit there's a chance that what the computer said could be right?"

"Yes, a chance."

"How much of a chance?"

"I have no idea."

"Come on! You must have *some* idea—your own personal feeling."

Terry paused to think. "My own personal guess is that if we published now, based on the way the world is today, the chances we'd end up destroying life are less than fifty percent. Fifty percent *tops*. But that's just my own guess. It might even be what we need to *save* ourselves! Or none of the above." Terry leaned forward on his stool. "Look, Mike, this isn't some kid's game. We stopped Worm from publishing, but we can't stop everyone. *Someone* is going to publish this theory or something very like it—and quite possibly will receive the Nobel Prize for it—and it might as well be us!"

"You'd be willing to risk an even chance of destroying the world—?"

"The theory will come out anyway! I've worked for this, and *I want that prize.*"

"It should make your mother very proud of you."

"Look, buddy, I didn't *have* to let you know about her. I could have let you sleep on a park bench last night!" Terry flared up so suddenly, he almost seemed like a different person. Then he controlled himself. "I'm sorry, Mike, I shouldn't have said that. It's just that you've done some really terrific work, and I think you deserve credit, that's all. I mean, this is something you should be *proud* to sign your name to."

"And if I don't, will it be published without my name?"

Terry looked at the floor. "Mike, just stop and think a minute about what this could mean to you. Publishing something like this at your age— why, you could write your ticket. You could do any research you want: they'd have to *respect* you. Someone like that dean at your college could never again deny you access to the research facilities you need. You could be set for life!"

It *was* a tempting thought. I could picture myself with an office and laboratory of my own, like Terry's, doing any research I felt like, being consulted by scientists throughout the world, being quoted in newspapers. I wavered a moment. Then I thought of the risk—to the whole world and, tied up in that, to me personally—and I knew I was just plain scared. It wasn't worth it. Nothing was.

We were down to the basic. I swallowed and looked Terry straight in the eyes.

"Those are *my* formulae, and *I* don't want them published."

"But Mike—"

I made my voice as hard as I could get it. "Just like you said with Worm. *They're my formulae.*"

Terry silently studied his shoes for what seemed like a long time. "Is that your final word on the subject?"

"Yes."

Terry looked up at me briefly and then returned his gaze to the floor. "I think you're making a mistake, Mike. But I won't use your formulae without your permission."

"Is that a promise?"

"Yes."

We were both quiet for a while. At last Terry broke the silence. "Well, I've got work to do, so I guess I'll see you later."

"Oh—sure."

Terry ushered me out the heavy metal door, just as Jim reappeared with a paper cup of coffee. I stood out in the hallway thinking. I had Terry's word, but somehow I didn't feel as if I had won.

11 The Letter

I walked back to Terry's house. His mother was polite, but I felt that she wasn't thrilled with me.

"Well, Michael, did you have a nice walk?"

"Uh, yeah, fine."

"Will you be waiting here for Terry? He may not be getting back until late tonight."

I could tell she was hoping I would say no.

"I think I will, thanks." I didn't know what I could do here, but I *did* know I couldn't leave Terry alone in Ohio with my formulae. Not just yet. I needed time to think.

"Oh. Well, make yourself at home. You must be hungry. Would you like some brunch? Or, I should say a late lunch by now."

"Oh, well, I don't want to be any trouble."

"No trouble. Terry took along a tuna salad sandwich this morning, so I made some extra. And Mike, please feel free to use the shower if you'd like. I hung up an extra towel and a wash cloth."

Talk about hinting. Well, it wasn't my house and I didn't have much else to do, so I tried to be gracious about it. I had a theory that her attitude wasn't really personal—she just treated me the same way she always treated Terry: like a brilliant little boy who will never be able to take care of himself. I'd had experience dealing with a similar attitude. I just tried to keep out of her way for the rest of the afternoon.

Terry was late again that evening. Mrs. Miller fussed over the meat loaf, fretting and adding more juice to keep it from drying out.

"It happens every night," she told me, "without fail. Terry's so wrapped up in his work all the time, it just seems beyond him to remember that dinner is at six, not seven. Every night without fail."

I wondered why she just didn't plan dinner for seven o'clock instead. But that would have meant giving in.

Terry made his entrance promptly at seven. "Oh, Mike, hi! I didn't know if you'd still be around or not." His greeting sounded way too hearty. There was something phoney about it.

"Well, here I am."

"Did you think any more about our conversation?"

"Yes, a lot. And the answer's still the same."

Terry nodded. "Well, I guess we'll have to get you to the bus depot first thing tomorrow morning and get you headed back to New York. Your mother must be worrying."

"She's *always* worrying. She's probably called out the police by now." I knew right away that I'd made a mistake.

"You mean your mother doesn't know where you are?" Mrs. Miller broke in. "Michael, I feel just terrible that I didn't think of this. You can use our phone right now to call her."

"Oh, no, that's okay."

"Michael, I'd feel much better if—"

"No, I was just kidding. She knows where I am," I said quickly.

"Please, Michael, I'd—"

"Really, it's okay."

Mrs. Miller gave me a long look. "Well, of course, Michael, it's up to you. Dinner is served."

"Oh, I'm sorry, Mom." Terry looked at his watch. "I have to write a quick letter first. I forgot all about it."

"But dinner's all dried out!"

"It'll only take a minute. I've got to get it in the mailbox before the last pick-up."

"Well, be quick, then."

Terry dumped his coat on the couch and bounded upstairs. His mother sighed and hung up the coat in the closet. I could hear a typewriter pounding in Terry's room. A few minutes later, Terry rushed down the stairs with a letter in his hand.

"Terry, take your coat!" called his mother.

Terry ignored her and ran out the door.

I don't know exactly why, but something about the way Terry mentioned it told me that that letter was important. I had to know what it said.

"I'll just wash up," I said. She grunted.

Instead of heading to the bathroom, I tiptoed upstairs to Terry's room. The light was still on, and the typewriter was sitting on his desk, but he hadn't left out a carbon copy of the letter. Possibly he hadn't even made one. I hastily opened a few desk drawers but didn't find anything. Terry *had* to be up to something, and there *had* to be a way for me to find out what. Suddenly I had a thought. Terry's typewriter was one of those new electric portables—the same kind my parents got me when I went away to college—the kind with the snap-out ribbon cartridges. Just maybe I was in luck . . . I was! Terry had used a film ribbon, the kind where the keys leave clear impressions like cut-outs on the black ribbon, so you can actually read every letter that's been typed. I snapped out the cartridge and stuffed it into my shirt, than ran down to the bathroom and loudly washed my hands. My heart was pounding.

A moment later Terry ran in the front door. Peeking around the corner, I could see him standing in the middle of the living room and hugging himself to warm up.

"I told you it was cold," said his mother. Terry didn't answer. "Come and get it."

I studied myself in the mirror. The ribbon cartridge under my shirt made an obvious bulge in my clothing. I tried every pocket I had, but it wouldn't fit. I even tried under my armpit, holding it in place with my T-shirt, but that was obvious, too.

"Michael, are you coming?" It was Mrs. Miller's voice.

I glanced hastily around the bathroom. I could

store the cartridge temporarily in the medicine cabinet, but it might be discovered. Where else . . . ? Of course! I opened up the tank in back of the toilet and dumped the cartridge inside.

Dinner seemed to take forever. After dinner, I pretended to be busy reading over computer programs, but actually I was just waiting for Terry and his mother to go to bed. That took even longer than dinner. Finally, around ten o'clock, they both hit the sack. I pretended to go to bed, too; but once we'd all been safely in bed for about a half-hour, I crept into the bathroom and locked the door behind me.

I rolled up my sleeves and fished in the tank for the ribbon cartridge; I knew that the water was sanitary, but the thought of it made me squirm and besides it was ice-cold. I dried off the cartridge and myself as best I could with toilet paper. If I had used my towel, I would have had to use the same one again in the morning, and I didn't like that idea.

I held up the cartridge to the light. On the inch or two of ribbon that was visible, I read 30606 sionil. I knew enough to read it backwards, which is the order the letters wind up in on the ribbon—linois 60603—but it still made no sense. I was expecting to see something like *D.bP,relliM* from *Sincerely yours, Terence Miller, Ph.D.*, but numbers? No, of course, it must be Illinois 60603, part of an address! Terry had typed the envelope after the letter.

I cracked open the cartridge and pulled out the ribbon. It was a mess—yards and yards long, and as limp and tangly as overcooked linguini. I soon had black, gritty smudges all over my hands and arms. It was tough going, reading backwards and without spaces between the words. To make matters worse, Terry wasn't a terrific typist, so there were plenty of typos. I made out a few words and phrases—*last minute, Neutron, the, Dear.* I finally found the beginning of the letter and started reading:

Robert Sandford, Ph.D.
Director
Technological Institute
Chicago, Illinois 60603

Dear Bob:

I'm writing to advise you that I will be changing my lecture topic for the Third Annual Symposium on Nuclear Physics. The new topic will be "New Formulae to Chart Time-Space Motions of Subatomic Particles During the Decay of a Neutron." Sorry to hit you with this at the last minute. Just over the past few days my researchers and I have confirmed some rather impressive new findings, and I'm eager to take this opportunity of presenting them to as many of my colleagues as possible. I do hope you'll be able to insert a notice of the change in the program, so the others will know to attend. Sorry again for the inconvenience. But once you hear the revolutionary nature of my lecture, I think you'll agree that it was worth it. See you in Chicago!

Sincerely,
Terence Miller, Ph.D.

I stared again at the new topic for his lecture. He was really doing it. In a few days, he'd be presenting my ideas to a hundred of the most influential scientists in the world. I felt a queasy feeling in my stomach. I'd really blown it. I never should have trusted Terry. I never should have told anyone. Somehow, at that moment I didn't think much about the possible deadly consequences for the world. I just thought about me. What really hurt was that Terry was stealing my formulae. My formulae. And there was nothing I could think of to do about it.

I cleaned up the bathroom and myself as best I could and dumped the ribbon and broken cartridge in the kitchen garbage bag, underneath a lot of other garbage. I couldn't get all the black smudges from my hand, arms, and face, but I didn't care. In a few days, all my work—perhaps the most important work I'd ever do in my life—would be for nothing. Terry would claim all the credit. And no one would ever believe me.

I went back to bed; and, for the first time since I was a kid at summer camp and my whole bunk had raided me, for the first time since then, I cried.

I was up and packed before Terry or his mother were even out of bed. I knew what I'd have to do now, at least in a vague, general way.

Terry drove me to the bus depot, in time for the New York bus. Apparently, he hadn't yet missed his ribbon cartridge. It wasn't a long drive, but it seemed like hours. The camaraderie and excitement we had shared just two days before were gone. Terry seemed older now, less like a kid. I couldn't believe that this was the same guy I had liked so immediately and talked with so freely, or that he was now betraying me. I felt like tearing him apart; instead I just stared straight ahead. Terry maintained an uneasy silence.

"You sure you won't reconsider . . . what we were talking about?" Terry asked hesitantly as we pulled into the depot.

I didn't answer.

"You got some number where I can reach you if anything comes up?"

I spoke my first words of the trip. "You can call the school. They'll know where to reach me."

Terry nodded. "Okay, Mike. Take care."

"Right."

Terry watched from the car as I bought the ticket I needed. Then he drove away.

Five minutes later the bus to New York departed on schedule, but I wasn't on it. I was in a phone booth calling Franklin College Student Information to get a home number. A moment later I placed my call.

"Worm! Can you get yourself some money and get to the airport? We're going to Chicago!"

12 Scouting Ahead

If I'd known I was going all the way to Chicago when I left Franklin, I would have taken a lot more money and made the trip by plane, as Worm did. But with the money I had left, I didn't have much choice. And if there's one experience I could have done without in my life, going from Ohio to Chicago by bus is it. You wouldn't think that just sitting would be such a hard thing; but when you have to do it on a bumpy bus, with the smells of gasoline and leather seats and some lady's sickening perfume, it's exhausting. And boring. I watched the scenery, made dumb conversation with the man sitting next to me (I told him I was visiting my grandmother), wrote a few equations, and read some junky novel I picked up at a rest stop. Mostly I just closed my eyes and waited for it to be over.

At least I didn't have to worry about time. I'd called Chicago before I left Ohio and found that the conference wouldn't be beginning for three days yet. That would give me about two days to recuperate.

The bus ride finally ended, and I took a local bus to Chicago University. I knew a few kids

from high school who went to school there, and
I was sure Worm did, too, so I was figuring that
one of them could probably put us up. But of
course, I'd forgotten that it was Christmas vacation; one look around reminded me of that as
soon as I hit campus. So I was in for a few more
nights at my favorite kind of hotel, conveniently
located near the institute where the symposium
was to be held. This one was called The Rialto
(ever notice how the sleaziest hotels have the fan-
ciest names?) and was about a step-and-a-half below Greenville's Plaza, if you can believe it. At
least this time I had an idea of what to expect,
and more important, I wouldn't be alone.

I checked in and went straight to bed. I needed
it. In the morning I caught another bus (I wished
I'd never have to see another) out to the airport
to meet Worm's plane. I got to the right gate a
little late and found Worm gazing around and
looking bewildered. I picked him out right away
from behind, even from the other end of the
building—I'd know his quirky, hunched walk
anywhere.

"Worm!"

"Mike!" He wheeled to face me, with a look
of immense relief.

"Did you think I was going to leave you
stranded?"

"No, I just. . . ."

I rushed forward to meet him and had to give
an awkward, sudden stop to keep from plowing
right into him. I never thought I'd be so glad
to see his tense, pimply face.

Worm started right in, as quickly as he could

get the words out. "Mike, I'm sorry about sending your formulae out to *Weekly Science Review*. It just never dawned on me—"

I waved his words away. "Yeah, so I went and gave them all to Terry Miller, which turned out to be an even bigger mistake."

"Right." It came out as kind of a husky croak.

"Hey, Worm—" I leaned forward, conspiratiorially. "So you and Margie actually ran the game through to the end?"

Worm's eyes lit up. "Yeah! You know, when I saw all those life readings dip to zero, I didn't know *what* was happening. I thought there were bugs in the program!"

"Me, too!" I piped. "Of course, I figured it out in a few minutes," I added quickly.

"Didn't take me very long, either."

We both burst out laughing.

"Bet it took me less time than it took you!"

"So what? I still won, prodigy!"

"Only once, genius. Wait till next time!" It felt good to be bickering with him again. I paused. "Actually, I'm glad you got so good at it, 'cause this time, you know, we're playing for real—you and me against Terry Miller."

Worm's smile faded. "Yeah. Mike, I still don't know what we're supposed to do or how I'm supposed to help you."

"Neither do I," I admitted. "But we'll figure out something together."

Worm bit his lip. "Um, I better warn you, Mike, I've had a little more experience with computer simulations than with real situations."

I knew that already. But I didn't say it.

"To be perfectly frank, this is my first time really out on my own like this. I mean, where do we stay, what do we do . . . ?"

I smiled. "Don't worry, I've taken care of everything. I got us a room at the Rialto." I liked the feeling of taking charge for a change.

"Great!" Worm smiled nervously. "I told my parents I was staying at a friend's house overnight. I don't know what will happen when I don't come back tomorrow."

"Don't worry, we should be out of here in a few days."

"That long?"

"Don't worry about it." I could tell he was worrying. "I think the bus was over this way."

I confidently led the way to the other end of the airport before realizing that we were hopelessly lost. A porter directed us to the buses, far away in the direction we had come from. At least we made it back to the hotel okay. Worm just looked bewildered by the new city. I smiled to myself. So, I was taking him under my wing for a while—if that's not too bizarre a figure of speech when you're talking about a Worm. Even with occasional mistakes, I had made significant progress in the art of finding my way around. I was doing at least a thousand percent better than I'd done at the beginning of the term.

The hotel was a dingy four-story building with a broken sign and a semiconscious old man sitting on the steps in front of the doorway. Worm took one look and bit his lip.

"Michael, you've got to be kidding."

"Wait till you see the room," I said.

He followed reluctantly. An extra bed had been moved in, as I had requested, shoved at a careless angle against a battered dresser. I made it a point not to look too closely at the sheets. A little pile of dust had appeared in the corner of the room, apparently somebody's idea of an adequate job of sweeping.

"Michael, you don't seriously mean for us to *stay* here?"

"It's not so bad. I picked it out myself. Conveniently located near the campus. . . ."

"Well, there must be someplace better."

"Okay. How much money have you got?"

"About fifty bucks."

"Forget it."

"Well, look." Worm took on his lecturing tone. "We pay about a hundred thirty dollars a month each for our room at Franklin, right? That's less than ten dollars a night for the two of us, in a new building. How much more can a half-decent hotel be?"

"You want ten dollars a day? You're looking at it."

"Well, if we pool our resources—it doesn't have to be anything fancy. How much have you got?"

"Eleven dollars and thirty-five cents. And we have to eat, stay a few nights, and have money for contingencies."

"Oh." Worm was quiet for a moment. He gave a nervous smile. "Well, thanks for finding us this swell place, Mike."

Smart-ass! Could he do any better? "We'll *manage*, Worm! We've got bigger problems to worry about now. Or did you forget about all that?" I was mad. Here he was supposed to be admiring my ability to cope, and instead he was picking at minor faults.

"Okay," Worm said in a small voice. He was quiet, almost penitent.

I got the feeling I'd been too hard on him. I swallowed. "Worm, thanks for coming all the way out here to help."

"Oh . . . well, that's the least I could do." He changed the subject. "So you think Miller's getting ready to spill it all at this symposium?"

"It looks that way."

"All right. How do we stop him?"

"I'm not sure."

We thought for a while.

"There's only one thing to do," Worm announced at last. "We shoot him."

"Brilliant."

"All right, I'm not seriously suggesting that. But the question is—what can we do short of that that will work?"

I didn't have an answer, but I thought out loud. "Well, if we could somehow prevent him from giving the lecture . . . But that would only be a temporary solution."

"Right. He'd still publish sooner or later."

"Still, this is *the* place to deliver a lecture like that. He kind of said that in the letter, that he wants to reach his colleagues at *this* meeting."

"You mean, like they're the guys to impress."

"Right." I was quiet a minute, then it hit me.

"Right! Worm, that's it! You've got it!" I *knew* Worm would help me think.

"Huh?"

"Worm, supposing he *doesn't* impress them? Supposing he slips up, makes such a bomb of his speech that no one will ever take the idea seriously again?"

"That's a thought. But how do we arrange that?"

"We could sabotage the speech—get to his notes, make a few changes in the intermediate steps of the derivation . . ."

"He'd have to notice. He must know his subject."

"But not that well. He told me himself that he's lousy at algebra. If he suddenly has to make corrections and figure quickly under that kind of pressure, it could be a fiasco!"

Worm looked dubious. "Mike, he *must* know algebra. The guy's a professor of physics!"

"So? So was Albert Einstein, but he couldn't do algebra to save himself. Don't forget, Worm, he's going to be under tremendous pressure up there, and we'll be springing this on him at the last minute. We'll be hitting him at his weakest point!"

Worm still didn't look entirely convinced. "It's a long shot, Mike." He considered some more. "But it could be our only chance."

"And we *still* have to figure out a way to do it. The conference doesn't start till tomorrow. I think we should use today to scout around— take a look at the places the different meetings will be, check out the schedule, see if there's anything that might help us get our hands on those notes."

"Sounds good to me."

We went downstairs, and I called up the institute to find out which hall the conference would be held in. Pierce Hall. We found our way to campus and asked directions to Pierce.

A security guard was sitting just inside the doorway. With the campus nearly deserted, I guess we were his big excitement for the day.

"You have some business here?"

"Uh, yeah, we have to pick up a term paper."

The guard nodded. "You mean you two guys are students here?"

"Yeah." Just what I needed, a suspicious guard. Maybe next time I'll get a phoney moustache to make me look older and avoid all the hassle.

"Can I see your ID?"

I glanced at Worm. "Sure." I supposed the college ID's all looked pretty much the same—maybe he wouldn't notice. We flashed our Franklin ID's, trying not to give him a good look at them.

"Just a minute," said the guard. "Let me see those." Worm and I glanced at each other again, then reluctantly held the ID's steady. No use getting the guard any more suspicious than he already was. He studied our photos, then our faces, then our photos again. He grunted.

"I guess it *is* you guys. All right."

We took back our ID's and walked in what we hoped was a casual way through the lobby.

A table was already stacked with schedules and other literature for the conference. I grabbed a copy of each, expecting to be challenged by the guard at any minute, and proceeded around the corner. Worm followed.

Worm let out a breath. "Well, at least we're in," he said in a low voice. "Let's take a look at the facilities."

We spent a half-hour or so wandering through the hallways, peeking in at locked conference rooms and lecture halls, using the schedule as a guide for the rooms we'd most likely need to know about. We got a feel for the layout of the place, but nothing gave us any terrific ideas for strategy. Pierce was just an ordinary classroom/office building.

We headed back to the lobby. "We'll just have to study this some more when we get back to the room," I was saying.

I became aware of the murmur of a familiar voice approaching from around the corner. I stopped short, listening.

"I really appreciate your accommodating this change. I'm very excited about what I have to announce. One could only call it revolutionary! As a matter of fact, one colleague of mine thinks it's *too* revolutionary. He's afraid it could be used for bad purposes, which of course raises some interesting ethical questions about scientific responsibility. But my view is that what I've discovered can be thought of as simply a power— a tremendous power that can be used for either good or evil. And I'm confident that ultimately the world will make the right choice. Now it seems to me . . ."

Terry and a smaller, older man turned the corner, their heads bent together in conversation. Terry was dressed in a freshly pressed business suit, looking more suave and professional than I'd ever seen him. He was so intent on finishing his thought that he hadn't even really looked down at us yet, even though he'd almost bumped into us.

I don't know what came over me. Before he even turned the corner, I knew it was him from his voice. I could have turned and run in the opposite direction before he even saw me. But I didn't. Maybe, somewhere, I wanted Terry to know that I was here and he wouldn't get away with it; or maybe I was just too surprised.

Terry looked down at us rather absently for the first time, turned back to his friend, then did a double take. His mouth opened.

"Mike!"

It was too late. I broke and ran through the lobby and out the door, with Worm close behind me.

"Mike! What are—"

The closing door cut off Terry's words.

13 An Almost Foolproof Plan

We didn't stop running until we were a few blocks away. No one came out of Pierce Hall to pursue us.

"That was him?" asked Worm when we stopped to catch our breaths. "The younger one?"

I nodded.

"So now he knows we're here. Great."

I still didn't say anything. I couldn't. For some reason I couldn't explain, I felt . . . *guilty*. It was as if I'd been caught in the act: as if I wasn't supposed to know that Terry was here, and because Terry was a grown-up and I was a kid, I had no right to fight back. It was ridiculous. Terry was stealing *my* formulae: and when I found him, *I* felt guilty. But that's how I felt.

"Mike, you all right?" Worm tugged at my shoulder.

"Yeah—yeah, I'm okay."

"Come on, let's get out of here. I'm freezing!"

Our hotel room wasn't all that much warmer, but it was out of the wind.

"All right, Mike. What do we do now?"

"Oh, just leave me alone a minute, will you?" Worm was quiet. There was plenty he could have said—"You got me all the way out here to *do* something, right? So let's *do* it, brainchild!" But he didn't; he just waited, sitting Indian-style on the bed. I was grateful to Worm for the reprieve, even if it *was* only for a minute. I didn't want to have to deal with the situation just then, but I knew I'd have to.

"Okay," I said when I felt I couldn't keep Worm waiting another second, "let's look at what we've got."

I opened up the printed schedule we'd picked up in the lobby. Stapled to the last page was a xeroxed sheet headed Changes:

Terrence Miller's paper, Improved Linear Accelerator Techniques, scheduled for 12 noon Tuesday, will not be presented. Dr. Miller will report instead on New Formulae to Chart Time-Space Motions of Subatomic Particles During the Decay of a Neutron. This report will take place at the same time as Dr. Miller's originally scheduled paper, but the place will be moved to Room 303 to accommodate a larger attendance.

Worm read the notice over my shoulder. "That's the report he can't make," I told Worm. "That gives us only tomorrow morning to sabotage his notes. He carries them around in a manila envelope." I opened the schedule to another page. "There's the morning coffee hour at ten and then lectures at eleven and eleven-thirty. Somehow at one of those three places, we have to get those notes away from him; if we can get them for just two or three minutes, I think we can do it."

"The only problem is, he'll be guarding them with his life." Worm made a sour face. "Especially now that he knows you're here."

"Maybe if I can create a diversion, you can get the notes. Or maybe he'll put them down next to his seat during the morning lectures."

"Or maybe he'll just hold them in his lap, and we'll be sunk."

"Well, *I* don't know! Do you have a better idea?"

"No," said Worm quietly. "I just think we should recognize that so far we really don't have any plan at all."

Worm was right, and I knew it. I looked down from Worm's face. "I'm sorry. I guess I'm just a little nervous about the idea of stealing his notes."

Worm smiled wryly, and then I did, too. The absurdity of the situation was evident: here Terry was endangering life on the entire planet, and doing so by stealing *my* formulae that *I* had invented, and *I* was worrying about taking his notes!

"It's our moral upbringing, Mike," said Worm. "It'll get us every time!"

We both started laughing, as much to break the tension as because it was really funny. I lay back on the bed and buried my head in the pillow; my laughter came so hard it felt almost like crying. "Moral upbringing!" I kept repeating it as if it were the funniest thing I'd ever heard of. Worm was sitting on the bed doubled over, giving his wheezy, almost soundless laugh. After a few minutes I controlled myself and sat up.

"Worm?"

Worm too regained his composure.

"Worm? What if we can't stop him?"

Worm shrugged his shoulders, then considered a moment. "Aah, we'll stop him, Mike. Hell, we can run a whole universe, we should be able to get around one nerd scientist!"

I laughed. After fighting alone for so long, it felt good to have an ally again. And I was glad that ally was Worm.

"All *right!*" I reached for my notebook and a pencil. "Let's put aside for a few minutes the question of how to get the notes and figure out what we do with them when we get them."

"Okay." Worm leaned forward to see what I was writing.

"Terry will probably be using a derivation something like this." I scribbled down some equations. "Somewhere around a third of the way through his figuring, he'll have to introduce some formulae like this, probably derived from his own observations. That's just before the figuring gets tough. If we change a few signs right over here, some terms will eventually drop out of the equation. We can let him get that far, change the signs, and then throw away the next two pages or so of calculations. Terry will have to struggle through all that figuring alone, without any notes, in front of an audience, and all based on a faulty premise that we'll have slipped in there. If he gets through the calculations without any further errors, which in itself is doubtful, he'll end up dividing by zero, and the whole equation will be meaningless!"

"Very neat!" Worm smiled in admiration. "And the clever thing is, as long as we only have to change some minus signs to plusses, he'll never notice the difference in handwriting!"

"Exactly! I think we've earned ourselves a lunch."

On the way out we stopped at a stationery store and stocked ourselves with a supply of practically every kind of pen and pencil they carried so we'd be sure to be able to match Terry's ink or lead color and avoid suspicion. Over our prefab hamburgers we considered further strategy. I remembered a James Coburn film I had once seen about a gang of pickpockets; Worm had seen it also. Using that as our inspiration, we devised our plan: I would bump into Terry and distract him. Worm, from behind, would switch Terry's envelope for a similar one that Worm would be carrying; he would hide his actions behind a coat, carried over his arm. We would then escape to a bathroom, alter the notes, and return to pull another switch so Terry would wind up with his own notes again. It was perfect, and scary, and exciting. Of course, usually the victims didn't know the pickpockets; but we decided that in this case, when Terry recognized me it would only make him all the more distracted.

We practiced all afternoon and evening in the

hotel room, taking turns at playing Terry while the other one of us practiced his own part. I would practice bumping Worm in different ways and ask him which was the most distracting. Then I'd be Terry and hold the envelope in all different positions and Worm would practice switching envelopes on me. When he asked, I had to admit that I *did* notice something going on, but we decided that the distraction of my bumping into Terry would take care of that. It would have been nice if someone else could have played Terry for us so that Worm and I could practice simultaneously; but, after extensive preparation, we felt confident that we could execute our operation flawlessly in the morning.

Just before bedtime, I scribbled in my notebook the exact alterations we would make in Terry's notes. I laid out the notebook, a manila envelope, and an assortment of pens and pencils, so nothing would be forgotten. Everything was ready.

Early next morning I woke up to a pounding at the door. If I'd been more awake, I never would have opened it; but I was still half asleep and didn't know what to expect, so I staggered out of bed and opened up.

A tall, beefy, middle-aged man in a heavy winter coat stepped right into the room and stood smack in the middle of the doorway, blocking it with his frame. He looked first at me, then at Worm—who was just beginning to focus—then down at me again.

"Mike."

"Yeah?"

He took in the room—the sagging mattresses, the peeling paint, the pile of dust and lint on the floor—and I could tell right away he didn't approve. Then I wondered, who's *this* guy to approve or disapprove? He extended his hand and took mine in a firm, painful handshake—the kind someone gives when he wants to show what a big strong man he is. I hate that. I winced and tried to pull away, but he just kept right on holding for about half a minute while he talked, as if he didn't know that he was hurting me.

"Mike, I'm Mr. Sheppard. Your parents hired me to find you and take you home again."

"What?" It took a minute the information to register.

"Get dressed, Mike. You're going home."

"But—but I can't now! Just give me till this afternoon. After one o'clock I'll go anywhere!"

"We're going *now*, Mike."

"But you don't understand—"

"Oh, I think I do." The smug jerk! He tossed me my clothes from the foot of the bed. "Get dressed." He noticed Worm staring silently up at him from under the sheets of the second bed. "Who's this guy?"

"Oh, he's just a friend. He lives here." I wondered how much Worm could see without his glasses on; if he'd be able to recognize Sheppard again.

Sheppard opened his coat. "I'm waiting, Mike."

"But *please*, it's *important!*"

He raised his eyebrows and gave me a bored look to show he wasn't buying it—and wasn't budging.

I took my clothes and walked into the bathroom—I had splurged on a room with a bath, such as it was—and closed the door behind me. I opened the window and immediately cringed at the chill that cut through my thin pajamas. I looked out. We were on the fifth floor, with no fire escape, no way to get out. I bet Sheppard must have checked all that out before he even came up after me.

Of all the rotten luck and rotten timing! Of all times to be kidnapped, and on the orders of my own mother! I got dressed as slowly as I could, trying desperately to imagine a plan of escape. Sheppard's voice droned through the door. "You know, your mother's worried sick about you, she's frantic—and your father, too! No word in nearly two months. She should see you now, halfway across the country, living in some flophouse!" I wondered what made him think he could talk to me that way. The arrogant bastard probably just assumed it was one of his God-given inalienable rights to lambaste anyone whose style of living he didn't like. "Folks work hard trying to put you through school, then have to spend it all on me instead . . ." I could tell it broke his heart to accept their money.

I finished dressing and walked back into the

room. Sheppard was still standing in the doorway; Worm was still in bed, but now he had his glasses on. Somehow he had looked almost naked without his glasses. I pulled on my coat and picked up my notebook. Then I sat down in the one chair at the far end of the room.

"I'm not going."

Sheppard looked at me reproachfully. "Michael . . ."

"I said I'm not going."

Sheppard sighed as if he didn't want to have to do it, then stepped toward me. I curled my legs under me, my feet tensed against the back of the chair. I let him get a step closer, so that the doorway was free—then I sprang, diving clear over Worm and the bed. Or, that was the idea, anyway. Actually I landed crossways on top of Worm, right on his stomach. Worm gave a startled "Oof!" I think I knocked the air out of him. And Sheppard grabbed me. I struggled and kicked to get away, but Sheppard just held me out at arm's length as if I were a doll; it was surprising and distressing how absolutely ineffective I was against him.

"You're only making things difficult, Mike." Sheppard spoke as if he were a well-meaning teacher and I a troublesome kid. Meanwhile I was still struggling while he held me in midair. I stopped fighting it. "Now wasn't that silly?" Sheppard returned me to the floor and placed his hands firmly on my shoulders; it was understood that he could get a lot rougher if I gave him cause. "Let's go, Mike."

"Just a minute." I turned to Worm, who was sitting up, making a heaving sound as he caught his breath again.

He smiled wanly. "Nice move, Mike."

"Sorry about that. You okay?"

"Yeah."

I gave Worm what I hoped was a meaningful look and pressed the notebook into his hands. He nodded and took it.

Sheppard's hands turned me firmly away. "Say goodbye, Mike."

He led me out into the hallway and down the stairs. Over my shoulder, I could see Worm watching us uncertainly through the doorway and holding the notebook tightly.

I didn't know if he could pull it off alone, but I was afraid he'd have to. It was up to him now.

14 No Way Out

The desk clerk looked at us quizzically as Sheppard marched me through the lobby, but he didn't say anything. Sheppard never took his hands off my shoulders.

"Could you get that for me, Mike?" Sheppard asked when we reached the front door.

I just stood there.

Sheppard sighed and tightened his grip with his right hand as he let go with his left to open the door. I bolted through the doorway—and was jerked back with a yank that made my shoulder feel as if it had just been pulled out of its socket. Sheppard steadied me with his other hand.

"Are you all right, Mike?"

I still didn't say anything.

"Mike, I don't want to have to be rough with you, but I'll do it if that's what it takes to keep you from running off. You're going back to your parents now, no matter what. It's not so terrible. They're nice people, believe me." I loved this—*him* telling *me* about *my* parents. "They're *worried* about you. So why don't you relax, and we'll have a pleasant journey together?"

I turned to face him. "If you just give me till one o'clock, I *will*—I *swear* it!"

Sheppard smiled. "And after one o'clock, where will you be, huh? Come on!"

It never fails: the one time you're telling the truth and really will keep a promise, a grownup will always think you're putting one over on him.

"How do I know it was really my parents who sent you after me?"

"Would you like to call them right now? There's a pay phone right on the corner. They'd be glad to hear from you."

"No, thanks." Talking with my parents was the last thing I wanted to deal with right then. I'd have to face that soon enough, anyway.

We approached a big, black car parked a few yards from the hotel. Sheppard marched me around to the driver's side, opened the door, and gently pushed me across to the passenger seat. Then he got in and closed the door.

The first thing I noticed was that the knob had been removed from the lock on my door and on the back seat doors as well; instead, there was just a hole with a little, pointed tip of a screw just barely sticking out through it. Hoping that Sheppard wouldn't notice, I tried the door; it was locked.

"That's for your own protection, Mike." Sheppard watched me out of the corner of his eye. "We wouldn't want you trying anything dangerous in traffic."

"Thanks."

For some reason, Sheppard seemed to find that hilarious. He chuckled loudly to himself.

As we pulled out, I caught sight of Worm watching helplessly from the fifth floor window. He'd have to pull the con on Terry all by himself now—Worm, who, while a brilliant computer strategist, was woefully inadequate at gauging personal interactions; Worm, who had so utterly fumbled our interview with Dean Stanley; Worm, who had so blithely sent my formulae to *The Weekly Science Review*. As I watched him, I felt a sinking in my stomach: he could never do it by himself. Never. I *had* to escape! I rattled the door handle and picked frantically at the screw from the lock until my fingers were bleeding. Nothing gave.

Sheppard seemed to watch out of the corner of his eye, but, curiously, didn't say anything. Soon we were on the expressway, but I had no idea of our route. I was fixated on the lock. Sheppard was quiet for a long time; then he took a long breath.

"It can't be done, Mike. All you're doing is tearing up your hands." He was right, but I didn't want to admit it. My fingers felt like chopped meat. "You know, your parents are paying me to bring you back in one piece. What'll your mother say when she sees those hands? 'Hey, you're trying to pass off damaged goods! Damaged in transit!'"

Just what I needed: a private eye who thought he was a comedian. I kept working at the lock.

"Is it really that bad, what you're going home to?" Sheppard tried to sound really concerned, giving me the big brother bit. I needed that even less than the comedy. "What are you running away from? Come on, you can tell me. Huh?"

"Nothing."

"It's gotta be *something*—or you wouldn't be running all the way out to Chicago, right? You wouldn't be sitting there tearing up your fingers on a lock you'll never open as if your life depended on it, right? So what are you running away from? Who are you afraid of telling: me . . . or you?"

Brother! Give me a break! How do you tell a guy like that that he's got his head screwed on backwards. Terry was probably putting the finishing touches on what could be the most destructive presentation in history while I was stuck in a car somewhere on the expressway with Sheppard! And still no way out.

"How did you find me?" I asked to change the subject.

"Well . . ." He smiled modestly. "That's my job."

As if it were so hard to figure out. Terry must have called Mom—probably got her number from Franklin—and let her know I was in Chicago so I wouldn't bother him. Then all Sheppard had to do was check a few hotels.

The expressway was moving more slowly now. Sheppard took an exit, probably hoping to get around the traffic—and drove right into a full-fledged traffic jam on the city streets.

"Oh . . . great!" Sheppard focused on the traffic clogging up ahead and slapped the dashboard. I think he was going to say something other than *great* and changed his mind when he remembered that I was there. In a few moments we had slowed to nearly a standstill; Sheppard honked (for whatever good *that* did) and muttered under his breath (which probably did even less).

Now I saw my chance. While Sheppard was preoccupied, I carefully rolled down the window—I timed the rolling to coincide with the honking so he wouldn't hear—and rose to my knees. Sheppard apparently noticed my movement and turned to look at me. It had to be now. We were going maybe five miles an hour. I stuck my head out the window and rolled out onto the road.

I scraped my hands and knees against the pavement as I landed, sprawled on all fours in the middle of the street. Cars behind honked and jammed on their brakes, but at the speed they were going, they wouldn't have had much chance of hitting me if they'd *wanted* to. I was up in a second and running to the sidewalk—my knees and hands stinging and a cool breeze coursing through the flapping shreds of the knees of my pants.

Sheppard must have been caught by surprise. I knew in a moment he'd collect himself and stop in the middle of traffic and come running after me, so I didn't stop to look. The cold air felt like sandpaper in my lungs as I dashed around a corner and ducked into an office building. I made it into an elevator just as the doors were about to close. The people inside stared

at me, but I didn't care. I got off on the second
floor it stopped at and caught my breath.

Down the block I could hear car horns blast-
ing. Sheppard had probably abandoned his car
in the middle lane to pursue me. He'd probably
assume I was on the street somewhere and run
around a few blocks, probably ask people if they
saw me; if that didn't yield anything, he'd have
to go back to his car pretty soon and park it
and then look some more. Even if someone *did*
tell him I went into this building, with any luck
I could get out again and miss him before he
could search every floor. I waited a few minutes,
then took the elevator down again, slipped
through the lobby, and peeked through the glass
doors—no sign of Sheppard. I ran a few more
blocks, putting as much distance as possible between me and the street we'd been driving on.
I looked at my watch: incredible! Nearly ten
thirty! I had only an hour and a half to find my
way back to the Institute and stop Terry.

I tried flagging down some cars to hitch a ride,
but no one stopped. I must have looked too much
like a fugitive. I had no money for a cab. All I
could do was ask directions and wait for a bus.
I hid in a store near the bus stop in case Sheppard
came by; the bus seemed to take forever to arrive,
although my watch told me I had only waited
ten minutes. Downtown I had to switch to another bus for the Institute. That one really *did*
take forever to come.

On the bus, I divided my attention between
my watch and signs of progress on our slow,

local route. We made every stop you could imagine. I tried to spur the bus onward with my thoughts and hold back the progress of the minute hand. At times it almost seemed to work, until I looked at my watch again. I asked passengers how much longer the ride should take. Too long. Too long, by just a few minutes. I could only pray that the symposium was running behind schedule. And even then I'd have only a few minutes to switch Terry's notes, if Worm hadn't already botched the job.

At last we reached my stop. I dashed off the bus and sprinted to the Institute. If the symposium were running late, I just might still make it.

As I rounded the corner to Pierce Hall, a tall, beefy figure suddenly loomed in the doorway. *Sheppard!* I stopped short, my heart knocking against my chest like the engine in Dad's car; I'd never make it by him! The man turned to take a bite from his sandwich, his eyes resting on me for a moment. . . . What *now?* All the air seemed to leave my body at once: no, it wasn't Sheppard at all, it was only some stranger of about his size and shape.

I wished I could cry for a moment, just to let out the tension, but there was no time. Time was everything now. My knees felt like Jello, but I forced them to start working again. As I raced through the door, I looked down at my watch: it was five minutes after twelve.

15 Down to the Wire

I took the stairs at a gallop, two or three at a time, and dashed to the conference room. The door was closed; I stood panting, looking through the little window. The audience was assembled, Terry was at the rostrum beginning his lecture. I was too late! In minutes, Terry would be insuring the cancellation of life on the entire planet. What was left? Should I rush the conference room, grab his notes, denounce him? Would it help? Would anything help?

A small movement toward the back of the conference room caught my eye: Worm! He gave me the high sign and smiled faintly. I was thunderstruck. Had Worm managed the switch by himself? I gave him a questioning look; he nodded.

How? How could he have done it?

Matching coffee stains on Terry's suit and Worm's shirt told the story. Worm had obviously bumped into him with some coffee and made the switch under cover of wiping up the damage. It would then be a simple matter to modify Terry's notes and then give them back to him, apologizing for the mix-up, just before his lecture. Worm watched my eyes and allowed himself a little bit more of a smile in self-congratulation: *Elementary, my dear Goldman.* He had done it.

It may sound funny, but I didn't feel grateful or even relieved. What I felt was . . . frustrated, disappointed, enraged. Here I had managed a daring escape, practically broken my neck racing there to save the world because I knew Worm could never manage it himself—and the ingrate hadn't even waited for me! He'd managed perfectly well for himself after all. I wasn't needed. It was such an anticlimax to the morning. I knew of course that Worm had done the only thing he *could* do under the circumstances, in fact what I myself had silently pleaded with him to do, but I suddenly felt so *useless.* Yes, Worm had followed *my* plan, making *my* alterations in Terry's notes, but it wasn't my show anymore: Worm had executed the plan himself.

Terry cleared his throat and shuffled his notes, ready to begin, and I was reminded that my worries were premature, to say the least. So the plan had been carried out. The big question now was, would it work?

Terry began his lecture and copied some equations onto the blackboard as he spoke, approximately the equations I had expected him to use. A pleased little smile played on his lips, and he looked confident and boyish again, the way he'd seemed when I first met him. I strained to make out his equations against the glare of the blackboard—so far, so good. As the equations progressed, Terry became more animated and enthusiastic, scribbling as fast as he could to keep up with his thoughts, overcome with the excitement of rediscovery. The scientists in the audience sat up with interest. There was no denying he was bright. Could I really expect to foil him with my little scheme?

The equations approached the crucial point. I held my breath, waiting to see what would happen; my shoulders felt as if they were tied in an aching knot. Now Terry introduced the new equation; he hesitated a moment in the writing, as if unsure about a detail. I didn't breathe. Then he copied it onto the board, with a plus sign where a minus should have been. We'd won! If he'd just keep going without question, we'd have him! He continued to the bottom of the page, then turned to his next page and stopped. An expression of panic crossed his face, like a kid caught without his homework. He riffled through his notes, apparently searching for the missing two pages; he didn't find them. Naturally. I nearly choked with suspense, trying to keep the giddy laughter from exploding within me. Terry's expression turned to anger. His eyes sought out Worm in the back of the room and stared at him; he knew. Worm, fighting a bout of giddiness himself, sank lower in his chair and glanced at me. Following the direction of Worm's look, Terry turned to the door and saw me for the first time. His eyes widened, as if he felt *betrayed*. I ducked under the little window and let out a burst of high-pitched, nervous laughter.

We had him! I could see it now: Terry stumbling helplessly through a morass of equations, making error after error, which his colleagues would correct for him with rapidly decreasing good will—until the climactic moment when the drift of the equation would be revealed and the zero would become apparent in the denominator. "No wonder you come out with such unorthodox, 'revolutionary' results, as you call them," an older scientist would thunder, "when you insist on dividing by zero!"

My fit of laughter lasted a minute and left me weak. I pulled myself back to the present and again peered through the window, expecting to see a visibly shaken Professor Miller. Instead, he seemed to have regained control and gave me a glance that I could only interpret as one of amusement.

"I'm sorry." He addressed the audience. "What I *meant* to write was *this.*"

Terry approached the blackboard and corrected the signs on the equation we'd altered, then continued working through his derivation. His eyes sparkled with a boyish merriment—a sense of victory—that only Worm and I understood. Worm buried his head in his hands; my mouth must have hung open like a mailbox. How could he have seen through it, when we'd planned it all so *well?*

I opened the door and crept to the back of the conference room. Scientists turned to stare at me, but it didn't matter now.

"I hope our young friend hasn't missed anything," said Terry with a charming smile. "I'll wait while you find a seat."

The audience laughed, and I hastily sat down next to Worm.

"What do we do *now?*" Worm whispered.

"I don't know. I think we've had it!" Heads turned in our direction. I lowered my voice. "But we've got to do *something!*"

"Mike, I've been watching these lectures. The derivations don't seem to be as important as the final results. Our only hope is to show somehow that your equations aren't true."

"But they *are!* We've tested them against every kind of data we've got, every variation we know of on the deterioration of a neutron."

"*Every* variation?"

"Yes!"

"You tracked positive decay particles, negative decay particles, matter, anti-matter. . . ?"

Worm rambled on for a minute, but I wasn't listening anymore.

"Worm, you're *brilliant!*"

He smiled modestly. "I *knew* that. What did I say?"

"Anti-matter! How stupid could I have been? Worm, we've been focusing so much on the deterioration of the neutron, since that's what Terry was working with, that we never thought to test out the formulae with *anti*-neutrons! If we can show that the equations don't hold for anti-matter as well as for matter, then the formulae can't be valid!"

"But didn't you already test for that in the last program you wrote at Franklin?"

"Yes and no—I think that's where the third equation must fit in!"

"The third equation?"

"Never mind about that now! Just run to the library and find me any data you can about the deterioration of an anti-neutron!"

"But I'll never make it!"

"Just do it! If you don't get back in time, I'll have to wing it, but *try!*"

Worm got up and slunk to the door, then let it slam loudly behind him as he sprinted down the hallway. People turned to give me dirty looks again or shake their heads, probably wondering why no one had yet thrown the two of us out.

Meanwhile, Terry was completing his derivation and demonstrating how the formulae fit his data. The figures fit neatly into place. The room was silent for a moment; then there were grunts of admiration, and scientists exclaimed softly to themselves. "Amazing!" "It really seems to work!"

Terry let himself smile all the way now: he owned that conference room. "And thus far, all the other hundred or so experimental values we've tested work similarly. Are there any questions?"

A few hands shot up. Several scientists tried to shoot the theory down with quibbles or minor discrepancies, but no one was able to hit at the crux of the thing. I held my breath, trying to will the questions to go on indefinitely until Worm could return with the data. Why couldn't he *hurry?* But after about fifteen minutes the questions and challenges petered out. The theory held. Members of the conference started to applaud. Some even stood up in their places while others were getting ready to rush over to Terry to congratulate him. Terry was beaming.

It was now or never. I raised my hand.

"Dr. Miller! Dr. Miller!"

No one seemed to hear me. Damn! Could I have actually blown it? I stood up on the chair, waving my hand frantically, like some girls do when they know the answer, and shouted as loudly as I could from the back of the conference room.

"Dr. Miller! Dr. Miller!"

People turned around. I shouted again in a high, insistent voice.

"Dr. Miller! *I have a question!*"

16 Endgame

A low chuckle swept through the audience. I'm sure they wondered what a kid like me could possibly have to say; they must have thought it was hysterical. As a matter of fact, everyone in the whole room was laughing—except for Terry. He gave me a big, friendly smile, as if he was the great professor and I was the little kid; but the smile had something anxious about it—it wasn't his usual boyish grin.

"Yes, Michael. What would you like to ask?"

My throat was dry. I swallowed to try to wet it, but my voice still came out as a squeak. "Dr. Miller, did you ever try out these formulae with data from the decay of an *anti*-neutron?"

"What?"

I repeated my question. A low chuckle started again in one corner of the audience, and this time the laugh wasn't at my expense.

Terry swallowed. "Well, uh, no. It didn't yet occur to me to do that. But I think the results should be very similar."

"Yes, I think they should, *if* the formulae are correct."

The audience laughed again. I definitely had some sympathy because of the David-and-Goliath factor; I milked it for all it was worth. I was talking a good game, but I'd still need the data to prove my point—assuming, of course, that my hunch was correct. Where was Worm?

"Well, I certainly have no objection to testing out the formulae against any available data, if we can find it," Terry said carefully. "I'm sure that after the conference we could look up the data and prove it out—"

"Why not now?" I piped. Again the audience laughed.

"Well, if we can find it quickly enough, but the next lecture is scheduled for—"

"I've got it!" Worm burst into the room, nearly heaving the door off its hinges, waving a few xeroxed pages in his hand. "I found it!" He handed the pages triumphantly to Terry.

Terry didn't put his hand out to take them. "What's this?"

"The data on anti-neutrons from last Spring's *Quantum!*"

The audience was buzzing now. I heard several voices asking at once, "Who *are* those kids?"

"Now you can test out the formulae!" I called from the back.

Terry looked around in confusion. Worm was still holding the pages in the professor's face, and Terry still refused to take them, as if even touching them might somehow legitimize them.

"You just hand me some xeroxed pages here

in the middle of a conference. I don't know where these pages come from."

"I told you," Worm persisted. "They're from *Quantum.*"

The scientist we had seen with Terry the day before came forward.

"Let me see that." He perused the pages. "Yes, Terry, I remember this article. And the results were duplicated just last month in West Germany."

"I know that, Dr. Sandford, of course," Terry said in a low voice. "But this is only a xerox. How do we know that those figures weren't tampered with when the page was copied?"

"Do you really think . . . ?"

Terry looked directly at Worm and me. "Some people *have* been known to use such tactics."

Dr. Sandford nodded. "I see." He raised his voice to address the conference. "Gentlemen, we're going to have a brief pause while I call the library to verify these figures. Please bear with us."

The audience hushed while Dr. Sandford picked up the interoffice phone and made his call. The buzzing started again when he finished; everyone wanted to know about "the kids," but they asked everyone but us.

In a minute a student appeared at the door with the Spring issue of *Quantum.* Dr. Sandford took it from him, thanked him, and handed it to Terry. "I think we can rely on this for our figures."

Terry took the magazine and nodded.

I looked at Worm across the room and gave him a tight smile; he returned it. It was a fair game now: my hunch against the formulae.

Terry copied out some of the data and started plugging them into his equations. It suddenly seemed so absurd, that the fate of the world could hinge on the outcome of two equations scrawled on a blackboard in a conference room in Chicago. Terry continued his figuring. I held my breath . . . and the results didn't match! The predicted value was far different from the one experimentally observed.

Terry bit his lip. He scanned his figuring for possible mathematical errors but didn't find any.

"Let me try another value here." He tried the formulae with another example. And stopped his calculations after only two steps. Scattered snickers sounded from the audience. It was obvious that the new results would be even farther off than the first example. Impossibly far off. Terry laid down his chalk and paused, then turned to face the conference. He studied the floor.

"I'm sorry," he said in a barely audible voice. "Apparently these formulae still require some more thought. I'm sorry to have taken the symposium's time prematurely."

One young scientist let out a laugh that sounded like a loud whoop; another clapped his hands twice in excitement. Most of the audience was laughing now. Ten minutes before, Terry was a *wunderkind*; now he was a fool.

Terry turned and rushed toward the door, but Dr. Sandford intercepted him and placed an arm on his shoulder, speaking to him in low tones. Terry wouldn't meet the older man's eyes; his face was bright pink.

I almost felt sorry for him. Well, all right, I *did* feel a little sorry for him, seeing him humiliated like that and everyone ganging up on him. I even felt a little guilty for having caused it. Then I reminded myself of what Terry had been trying to do and what could have happened if he'd succeeded; and I knew that what I'd done had been necessary.

I'd seen enough of the symposium. Before the scientists could congratulate me and ask who I was, before they could start fawning on me for showing up their colleague, I slipped through the crowd and out into the hall—just as Terry broke away from Dr. Sandford and escaped through the doorway. He caught sight of me and stopped short, fixing me with an angry, hurt stare.

I colored. "I'm sorry, Terry."

"You're sorry. After ruining my career—and your own . . . !"

I looked him right in the eye. "You stole my formulae. You had no right to do that. I trusted you, Terry."

Terry's eyes welled with tears. "I was willing to share. Those formulae applied to my research represented work from *both* of us! We could have worked out the difficulty together!"

"You still stole my formulae."

Terry seemed about to hit the wall with frustration, but he didn't. He controlled himself and put on a strange, bitter smile that didn't look much like a smile. "Some day you'll realize what you did, Mike, what you gave up. And then it won't do any good. Maybe you already know how to make those formulae work. Maybe you've already figured out some little twist in the equations that will make them come out right. Well, maybe someone else will figure it out, too. It might even be me, if they'll listen to me again. And if not . . . well, somewhere in that room, Mike, a scientist was listening to what I said and thinking about it. And when he gets home, he's going to think about it some more, figure out what the mistake was, and publish his theory. The only difference will be that he'll get the credit, not you or me."

"That might happen. Or it might not."

Terry looked at me in disgust. "You *had* to ruin it, didn't you?"

"Yes. I had to."

Inside the conference room, the audience was buzzing and beginning to head for the door. Terry abruptly turned and disappeared down the hallway before the first of them left the room.

In a moment, the crowd poured out. Some were laughing, others were shaking their heads. Worm fought his way through the clogged doorway. He rushed toward me, his face glowing with relief and success. He looked as if he were ready to jump out of his shoes—and suddenly I felt the same way. Against all the odds, we'd managed, and the world was safe.

"We did it!" I yelled as Worm approached,

and suddenly, with a simultaneous impulse, we caught hold and hugged each other. We hung on as doggedly as if to let go would be to let the world careen again toward disaster. The scientists coming out of the room stared at us, but we didn't care; we just hung on and laughed wildly.

17 Unfinished Business

"So does that mean the formulae were wrong after all?" Worm asked on the way back to the hotel.

"Not wrong," I explained. "Only incomplete. You remember I originally wrote the formulae as three linked equations."

"Right."

"But when I played around with them some more on the bus ride to Ohio, I thought I saw a way to simplify things—a way I could reduce the formulae to only two equations and still get the same results. I was so taken with the elegance of that, that I lost sight of the reason I'd written that third equation in the first place: to take into account situations precisely like this one, the tracking of anti-matter."

"And all Terry ever saw was the two-equation version of your formulae."

"Exactly!" I laughed. "I never thought I'd be so glad to make a mistake!"

Worm smiled. "Well, it's a good thing *I* was thinking about anti-matter at the conference, even if *you* weren't!"

That grated. "Yeah, I guess it is." I hated to admit that I'd needed Worm: but he was right, without him at the conference, I might never have found the way to stop Terry. Well, we had won, that was the main thing. I guess sometimes you can't do everything yourself. Independence is one thing, but sometimes you have to rely on other people to help you out. Terry had turned out to be the wrong person to trust for anything. But Worm had come through for me. And more than once, despite my doubts about him. I realized I'd have to think some more about who to trust and who not to.

We got our things from the hotel room and settled up our bill at the desk—with Worm's money, of course, since I was broke—and turned to see Sheppard standing behind us. He must have been watching from across the street or something, all set to pull some kind of surprise-and-capture routine. But I wasn't exactly shocked or even unhappy to see him. He looked rumpled and angry from chasing after me.

I giggled. "Hello, Mr. Sheppard. Can we give Worm a lift, too? I think he'll be taking the same plane as we are."

If I somehow could have gone straight back to Franklin, without ever stopping to see my parents, I would have done it. I had no desire to go through a whole scene with them. But I didn't have much choice under the circumstances, and I figured I owed them at least an appearance before school started again. I just hoped they wouldn't get *too* hysterical.

Mom and Dad met us at the airport. I felt
like a condemned man as I walked to the recep-
tion area and caught sight of them. Dad was pac-
ing and looking at his watch: Mom was straining
with an expression of pained anticipation, as if
she were certain that the plane had crashed and
no one had yet had the nerve to break the news
to her. Then she caught sight of me and started
laughing and crying at the same time and ran
to me. Dad waited his turn and Sheppard looked
on with an appearance of modest satisfaction.
Mom held me so tight I could hardly breathe.

I was touched at how glad she was to see me,
even if it *was* more than a little embarrassing;
even Dad looked relieved. I really hadn't *meant*
to get them so worried and upset; it was just
that once I was away at school I really didn't
want to have to deal with them and their crazi-
ness, their over-concern. But I hadn't meant for
them to take it like this. If they could just *let
go* a little bit, maybe we could work something
out.

That thought lasted about two minutes; then
they opened their mouths. How could I do this
to my mother? Didn't I know how worried they'd
been? Et cetera, et cetera. I quickly decided I
was very glad that I'd be returning to Franklin
in just a few days—a move they finally allowed
only with the greatest reluctance, and only on
condition that I give my sacred promise to call
Mom twice a week without fail, Monday and
Thursday evenings at seven o'clock sharp, of-
tener if I felt I needed to. It wasn't the best of

conditions, but it was a considerable improvement over living under the same roof with them, and it was something I could live with.

I got back to Franklin a day late for the new term. Buzz was the first one to see me on the dorm floor. I hadn't really given any thought to facing him again; but now that I did, I thought back to our last few conversations and felt awkward and a little ashamed. I wondered if he were still mad at me.

He was on his way to the elevator and I had just stepped off it, so there was no avoiding him.

"Hey! Hey, Mike. After last term, I wasn't sure whether I'd be seeing you around here or not!" He didn't seem displeased to see me.

"Yeah, well, for a while, neither was I."

"So, did you work out whatever it was you guys were working on?"

"Yeah, we did. Thanks." I wondered if I should say anything more, then decided I might as well, and stumbled on with it. "Buzz, I'm sorry if I was kind of taking your help for granted before. I, um . . . you know . . . and . . ." I didn't know what else to say. My ears burned. I felt like a jerk. "I thought you might have been mad about that."

"Well, now that you bring it up, I was, kind of." It wasn't exactly what I hoped I'd hear, but, as he said, I'd brought it up. "It wasn't just that. I felt like—well, kind of like you'd use me for messages and stuff when you needed to, but that otherwise you really didn't want to bother with ordinary people. Like maybe you were looking down on me."

"Oh." It was a lot to assimilate. I thought of arguing or of claiming to have been misunderstood. But something about what he said rang true. "I'm sorry I was like that."

"Well, that's okay." He punched me lightly on the shoulder. "Gotta run. Catch you later!" Buzz disappeared into the elevator.

My breaths were short, and my heart was pounding—all over a little apology! Still, it hadn't been so bad after all. Not the kind of thing I'd want to have to do every day, but I had survived.

I walked down to my room and got embarrassed all over again: the door was still decorated with the sign that read "CHILD PRODIGY TRAINING CENTER. Apply Within." I cringed. How could I have left that dumb thing there all semester? I tore down the sign and threw it into the garbage, hoping no one would notice.

Worm was sitting cross-legged on his bed when I entered the room, in front of our Absurdities wall. He looked up from his book and smiled warmly.

"Hi, Mike. Glad to see you!" He tossed me an official-looking envelope from the Dean's Office. "One for you and one for me."

I opened the envelope: we were beginning the term on academic probation. I wasn't surprised.

Probation wasn't really so bad, now that we had finished with our UNIVERSE PRIME game. The worst part was that we had only the most cursory access to the computer center, for prescribed course work only. In our spare time, though, we could console ourselves by planning the new games we would invent next year, when we would elect four credits of Independent Study in Computer Sciences—and by studying in detail every last print-out, no matter how trivial, that we had managed to extract on UNIVERSE PRIME.

Still, it *was* frustrating to have to shelve all our plans until the fall.

"You know, sometimes I wonder if it was all worth it," I remarked to Worm one afternoon as we went over our last bits of UNIVERSE PRIME data.

"If what was worth it?"

"Fouling up Terry. If I'd published with him, the way he wanted, I might have my own laboratory by now. At the least we'd be off probation. Nobody could tell us what we could or couldn't study. We'd have access to computers: we could program anything we wanted."

Worm smiled. "It's a nice dream. But of course, you're not forgetting why you decided *not* to publish with him."

"I know." There was something I'd never admitted before. "But sometimes I wonder if maybe Terry was right."

"How?"

"Well, maybe UNIVERSE PRIME *wasn't* such a close replica of the real world. Maybe dangers in UNIVERSE PRIME don't have to be the real dangers. Maybe it's just a game, as Terry said, that can suggest some possibilities but not all. Maybe we did it all for nothing."

"Beats me," said Worm.

I returned to the print-out before me. Some time near the beginning of our work, we had programed the computer to analyze portions of the Manhattan phone directory for the principles of people's names in English, and then to use those principles to generate the names of the one thousand citizens of WORM FARM. We had further instructed the computer to name the laws of the physical and social world after the citizens who had discovered them. What I had before me was a print-out of those thousand names and the names of the laws. We had never really made use of the list in our programing, and it did not promise to be among the most significant data to derive from UNIVERSE PRIME. As I scanned the list, one line caught my eye and made me sit up straight on the bed.

"Hey, Worm—look at this!"

Worm looked over my shoulder at the line I pointed to; his eyes got wide. Among the physical laws was an early draft of my time-travel formulae. And there, next to my formulae, was the name "MILLER-GOLDMAN EFFECT."

"I don't get it!" I exclaimed. "I never programmed my name into the computer, not that I can think of. And I certainly never programmed Terry's. We did this list weeks before we incorporated *The Weekly Science Review* into the program, before we even *heard* of Terry Miller!"

"So, the question is, how did the computer know that you and Terry even existed, let alone that you were the ones who were developing the time-travel formulae?"

"Exactly!"

Worm frowned. "We *did* program UNI-VERSE PRIME to parallel the real world."

"Well, yeah—in broad outline! But this kind of detail! It's almost as if the computer is filling in the blanks, going ahead on its own initiative, making even more detailed parallels than we ever thought of—and doing it with data we never even gave it! But that's impossible. . . !"

Worm gave me the smile he usually used when he was putting me on; he made his voice hollow and spooky. ". . . Unless there's more to this game of ours than even we imagined!"

I considered a minute. "Aah, it's probably just a coincidence. Miller and Goldman aren't exactly the most uncommon names in the world."

"Maybe." He again perused the print-out. "But nevertheless, it makes you wonder."

Worm was right. It made me wonder.

About the Author

A native of Great Neck, New York, Sandy Landsman began making up stories before he could write. During his senior year at Columbia, he launched an eleven-year career entertaining at schools and children's parties. He wrote and starred in his own children's cable T.V. show. In 1977, Mr. Landsman's children's musical, *Rake's Alley: A Musical for Cat Lovers of All Ages* was produced locally to good notices. For the past several years he has been a member of Margaret Gabel's Workshop in Writing for Children. THE GADGET FACTOR is his first published novel.

Great Science Fiction from SIGNET